The WHIMSICAL GIFTS of EMMA

BOOK ONE OF THE GIFT SERIES

ANITA FONTEBOA

To God, my angels and guides, thank you.
To my children, this book is dedicated to you. If mom made her
dreams come true, then you can too.
To my sister, thank you for listening.
To my husband, thank you. You have supported all my wins. I
love you.

PROLOGUE

—————————

WHERE THE MAGIC CAME FROM

In the Paz family, where generational magic flows, little did they know that little Emma would possess a unique, whimsical magic that would enchant.

It all began with Anita Paz, the family's matriarch. Anita had a quiet strength and warmth that radiated from her, a reflection of the wisdom gained through her life's challenges. Her brown skin spoke of countless days spent working in the fields under the sun. Her wavy brown hair framed her face and fell gently over her shoulders, complementing her brown eyes, which seemed to hold the wisdom of her life's struggles and triumphs.

Today, she wore a simple, earth-toned dress made of sturdy fabric that had seen many years of hard work. The dress was modest but well-kept, reflecting her humble nature. Anita was known throughout the village for her unwavering commitment to helping others. Despite growing up as an orphan in the small town of Higüey in the Dominican Republic, she always extended a helping hand to those in need, embodying the spirit of kindness and resilience.

Anita worked in the fields and often shared the fruits she gathered to fill up the baskets of other families who needed the money, even if it meant she would have less for herself. She would also assist elderly individuals by washing their clothes because they were unable to do so themselves. Despite challenges, Anita possessed a resilient spirit, never allowing anyone to bully her. Her resilience was evident, yet her selflessness did not go unnoticed. Watched from above, forces saw her actions beyond.

One crisp autumn afternoon, as the sun hung low in the sky, casting a warm, golden light over the landscape, Anita made her way down the path to the river. The air was cool and tinged with the earthy scent of fallen leaves. She wore a simple, faded cotton dress, its hem brushing against her ankles as she walked, and a wool shawl draped over her shoulders to ward off the lingering chill. The laundry bundle was securely balanced on her hip.

As she neared the riverbank, she could hear the gentle flow of the water mingling with the rustling of the dried leaves underfoot. Suddenly, a splash broke the calm, followed by desperate cries for help.

"Help me! Someone, please help!" The woman's voice pierced through the peaceful afternoon as Anita went down into the water. Her sharp eyes caught sight of a woman in the deeper part of the river. Her flailing hands and frantic arm movements showed she was desperate to escape as she struggled to stay afloat.

Anita looked around for anyone who could help, but saw no one nearby. Without hesitation, she dropped her laundry and removed her shawl, running toward the river before jumping into the water. Her dress clung to her as she swam with strong, practiced strokes, her focus on the woman. Anita swam behind her, securing a firm grip around the woman's waist.

"I've got you," Anita reassured, her voice steady despite the adrenaline coursing through her veins. With powerful kicks and unwavering resolve, she guided them both back to the riverbank, her breath visible in the chilly air as she fought against the current to bring them to safety.

As they reached the shore, the lady turned to Anita and said, "Thank you for saving me. I knew you would help me, but I wanted to test you."

Anita looked at the woman with confusion. "Who are you? And test me for what?" she asked.

The woman standing before her was dressed in tattered rags, and her dark brown skin bore the marks of hardship. Her long, dark brown hair cascaded down her back in tangled waves. Despite her destitute appearance, her voice carried a profound power and serenity.

"*Soy La Virgen de la Altagracia*," she declared, and as she spoke, her form began to change. A brilliant white light enveloped her, and her olive-toned skin seemed to glow with a divine, golden luminescence. Her ragged clothing transformed into a resplendent robe, and her once disheveled hair now flowed gracefully, embodying the mother of Jesus.

Anita went down on her knees in awe. She was speechless at the miracle unfolding before her.

"My child, I will bless you with gifts," said *La Virgen de la Altagracia*. "You will receive clairvoyance, allowing you to see beyond the physical realm, clairaudience, which will open your ears to the whispers of the universe, clairsentience allows you to feel the emotions of those around you, and claircognizance gives you the gift of knowing. Additionally, you will receive clairolfaction, which allows you to smell things that others cannot, and clairgustance, so you to taste the essence of things."

Anita was surprised and humbled by the revelation. "I have been chosen to receive these gifts because of my actions?"

"*Sí, mi hija*," *La Virgen de la Altagracia* replied. "Your lineage holds great significance, and these gifts will be passed down through your family to help more people."

Anita felt a sense of responsibility and gratitude wash over her. She knew these gifts were of great importance. "And what must I do with these gifts?"

"You must use them for good, my child," *La Virgen de la Altagracia* replied. "If you use them for evil, they will be taken away. And if your ego becomes too large, they will be removed."

Anita nodded, understanding the weight of the responsibility the gifts carried.

"And one more thing," *La Virgen de la Altagracia* said, "You must tell your family and their future families this story. They must know the truth of what happened here today."

Anita understood these gifts were sacred and carried a profound responsibility. She knew they must be used for good, and using them for evil meant she would lose them. She learned to control her ego because she could lose her gifts if she became vain and self-centered. With this knowledge, she embraced her role as a guardian of her family's legacy and the sacred gifts bestowed upon her.

Throughout her life, Anita passed down the story of her encounter with *La Virgen de la Altagracia* to her descendants, ensuring they understood the importance of humility, integrity, and the sacred nature of the gifts handed down to them. Each generation incorporated these teachings into their understanding of the family's history, honoring Anita's legacy, and the divine nature of the blessings she received.

CHAPTER 1

SEEING THE SPARK

It was a late Sunday afternoon, and the sky, once clear and blue, had begun to darken as a fresh rain shower moved in. The sun was hidden behind a blanket of gray clouds, casting a soft, diffused light over the room. The scent of rain and wet earth drifted in through the slightly open kitchen window, creating a calm and serene atmosphere.

Tía Fatima gathered her loose brown strands of hair and secured them with a clip. She had put on a colorful apron over her lilac floral dress to protect it from stains as she fed Emma. Spoon in hand, Fatima cooed and made funny faces at Emma in her highchair as she wiggled excitedly.

"Now open your mouth wide," Fatima said with a playful grin, making rocket noises to entertain Emma. With her head tilted and eyes wide, Emma opened her mouth, and Fatima expertly guided the spoon to her lips. Emma's eyes sparkled with delight, and Fatima's face lit up with a smile of pure joy.

"*Mira*, Ariana," Fatima called to her younger sister, who was standing nearby. Ariana wore a soft, mint-green dress, and her brown hair, styled in gentle waves, was adorned with butterfly hair clips. As she stepped closer, she crinkled her nose slightly and adjusted her glasses, their lenses reflecting the dim afternoon light. Her face, with its soft lines and gentle wrinkles, hinted at the wisdom of her years.

"Yes. I see it, too," Ariana agreed.

"What?" Mary, Emma's mother and Ariana's daughter, asked. Her light brown eyes followed the interaction between *Tía* Fatima and her mother. Mary had quickly changed into a soft peach sweater and matching lounge pants. Her hair was pulled back and tucked behind her ears. She managed to freshen up while juggling the demands of her busy household. Mary watched with a mixture of relief and appreciation, blessed to have an aunt and mother who could provide her with a much-needed break.

The conversation paused as Emma's cries grew louder, her hunger clear. Mary's eyes widened with empathy as she stepped forward and cleared her throat softly, a gentle but noticeable sound meant to capture Fatima's attention.

"Sorry, *mi chiquita*," *Tía* Fatima murmured soothingly, bringing the spoon back up to Emma's mouth. She turned to Ariana. "We must finish feeding the baby first," she said, her voice soft but firm, as she continued to feed Emma.

When Emma was done eating, *Tía* Fatima and Ariana opened the highchair to take her out. She rubbed her back, coaxing out any gas that had built up in her tummy. Fatima watched them walk around the room for several minutes before they heard an enormous burp from the baby. Startled, Emma opened her hand and out fell a white feather, and her eyes drooped as she drifted off to sleep on Ariana's shoulder.

Mary looked at the two women. "Now, are you going to tell me what you saw?"

Her mother and aunt exchanged glances, and Fatima raised a finger to her lips to show they needed to keep quiet so they would not wake Emma.

"Why don't you put her down for a nap?" Fatima suggested.

"OK," Mary said softly, heading to the bedroom to prepare everything.

She laid a fresh diaper on the changing table, along with baby wipes, before carefully removing a soft yellow swaddling suit and placing it on the table with the front open. Her mother arrived, carrying Emma, and gently laid her down on the changing table to undress and change her. She then securely fastened the diaper's tabs over the baby's chubby legs and zipped the swaddle suit up to her chest. After removing all of Emma's toys from the crib, Mary gently placed Emma down in her crib and twisted the knob on the mobile bar, and it began to play a soft lullaby. She switched on the monitor before exiting the room with her mother.

"Now, will you tell me?" Mary prodded.

"Shh ... soon," her mother said, and they watched for a moment from the door as Emma lay peacefully inside her crib.

Back in the kitchen, the two older women nodded somberly.

"We need to talk," they said.

They could hear Emma babbling away and laughing through the monitor in her crib. She had woken up. Mary knew she had a pacifier, and through the monitor's camera, she could see Emma's teddy was held firmly against her chest. She kept making funny faces at it while drumming her toes on the crib railing. She was a content baby.

Emma's vibrant giggles echoed from the baby monitor throughout the end of the house.

Her aunt and mother stared at her and said, "She has it!"

Mary started. "What does Emma have? Why do you keep saying that?"

Tía Fatima spoke first. "I was feeding her, and the sparkle in her eyes was unmistakable. She has the gift." She glanced over at Ariana, who nodded vigorously.

"*Mi hija*," her mom said softly, tears brimming. "I saw the glimmer in her eyes, too. She has the gift."

Mary went still as their words sank in. Remembering her mom's voice from long ago, telling the story of their gifted ancestors.

"We'll always be here for you as she grows and develops her gifts." Her mother and Aunt Fatima stood together, assuring her.

Mary looked from one to the other, overwhelmed by their kindness and support. She took a deep breath and replied, "*Gracias*. I know you will."

Afterward, while her aunt and mother tidied up the kitchen and living room, she folded the laundry, allowing herself time to process what they had just told her as she worked. Soon, she walked toward Emma's room with piles of freshly laundered clothes. The baby monitor beeped in her hand as she heard a light hum coming from inside the room. Hesitantly, she pushed open the door.

A bright, blinding light engulfed her, and she felt a strange breeze blow past her face, carrying the scent of flowers. She squinted, trying to adjust her eyes.

The light disappeared as quickly as it had come.

What just happened? she pondered. As she went to put the

clothes away in Emma's drawers, she spotted three white feathers resting next to Emma's pacifier. She crossed over to the crib. This was an absolute mystery. They had not been there before. She picked up one of the feathers and knew that something divine was in the room. It was an angel.

She reviewed the security footage, but all was clear. She could not see who put the feathers there. But she had felt something divine as she stood in the blinding light when she entered the room. The light. The feeling of something divine. The feathers.

For the first time, she, too, could sense that her daughter was different. Her knowing told her so. The room went silent as she picked up the other two feathers and held all three of them close to her chest. She closed her eyes in delight, and peace and love flowed through her body.

Her mom and *Tía* came into the room.

"Look at this," she said, holding up the three feathers.

They both gasped and stepped back.

"You can feel the spark in the room," her mom whispered in awe.

They all stood still, feeling the divine energy radiating from the feathers.

The sun peeked through the clouds, casting warm rays of sunlight through the window. A sense of anticipation hung in the air, mingling with the faint scent of lemon. Emma peacefully slumbered in her crib.

They quietly left the room.

Tía Fatima cleared her throat. When she spoke, her voice was soft yet commanding in the room's stillness. "Mary, Ariana, come sit," she said, gesturing toward the worn living room sofa by the fireplace.

Ariana tilted her head slightly, approvingly, her eyes reflecting the candle's flickering flame as she settled onto the cushions beside Fatima. Mary followed suit, her heart fluttering with stunned curiosity and apprehension.

"Ariana, remind Mary of the story since she appears to have forgotten," Fatima prompted her younger sister, her gaze shifting between the two women.

Ariana took a deep breath, her voice steady as she began to speak. "It's a story passed down from my *abuela* and her *abuela* through generations of our family," she explained, her words carrying the weight of centuries-old wisdom.

Fatima locked her eyes with Mary's as Ariana retold the story of Anita Paz and the legacy of the gifts bestowed upon their family.

Mary saw that *Tía* Fatima's eyes shimmered with awe and perhaps a bit of pride as Ariana spoke the final words of the tale. "Each adult in our family has been blessed with these gifts: a sense of knowing and visions of the future. Each person has different abilities, but they were all passed down from Anita to you, us, and now to Emma."

Mary had felt her own heart swell with pride and honor as she'd listened to her mother.

"But with these gifts comes great work," Ariana added, her voice tinged with solemnity. "They must be used wisely, for the greater good of all, to protect and guide."

Tía Fatima placed a reassuring hand on Mary's shoulder. "Emma's gifts will be a testament to our family's legacy of love, courage, and unwavering help to others."

Mary felt a renewed purpose as they sat together in my living room. She needed to be reminded of the Paz matriarch, Anita Paz, and how she came to possess the gifts passed down through generations. As she listened, she understood that Emma's path would not be easy. But with the strength of their family's bond and guidance, she would face whatever challenges lay ahead, united in their destiny, shared with the first woman of their family to have the gifts.

Mary closed her eyes and embraced the feathers, understanding Emma's calling. "My little girl will be magical, just like me."

Chapter 2

Meet Angel

Ever wish you had your own angel? Well, meet me.

My name is Angel, and I have been assigned to Emma. My job? To aid her in making choices that will guide her through her life's path. Yes, you heard it right. I am the one who helps her see the bigger picture, nudging her toward choices that align with her life's contract. Curious? Let me shed some light on what my job as her helper angel really is.

You see, I am not just assigned to Emma; every one of you has access to your own helper angel. When you pray for a parking spot, there is a helper angel assigned to assist you. When you ask for help with an idea or solution to your challenge, there is a helper angel. Are you seeking help with finances, health, or career guidance? That is where we come in. There is a helper angel for all of it. Think of us as your life coach, dedicated to helping you fulfill your unique purpose on this earthly plane.

We, as angels, come in various shapes and sizes. We have a sense of humor and can be stern with you. Our main job is to help you. You may have encountered us on the street, disguised as a homeless person, a lost child, or a frail elderly woman who needed a hand with her shopping bags. Or as someone you stopped on the street to get directions from when you were lost.

You can run into an angel and not know it because we are here to comfort and reassure you and to let you know that you are not alone, even when you do not believe it. When you feel alone, say a quick prayer, and you will be surprised at the answers you will receive. The message can be in the form of a picture, a song, or a message appearing on a television commercial or show on your screen.

I want you to know there is goodness in the world, and it is filled with love. However, there is also a darkness that may try to make you feel alone and create doubts in your heart. You can combat this negativity by raising your vibrations, meditating, and cleansing the space around you. Once you connect, the darkness cannot feed off your fear, because you will be in the realm of love and cannot be touched.

Let's distinguish between archangels, helper angels, and guardian angels. Archangels are considered super angels, with Archangel Michael being known as the leader of God's army and a defender of those in need. Guardian angels are celestial beings who protect you from darkness and guide you on your life's path. Helper angels, on the other hand, are spiritual beings present to light up your path and empower you to make decisions in line with your soul's purpose. It all comes down to tapping your inner wisdom and connecting with the divine guidance that surrounds you.

As I mentioned, my mission is to guide Emma through her life's purpose, just as I do with my caseload of many other souls across different galaxies. Her life's purpose is unique to her, as each of you has your own purpose. My job is to ensure that she stays on track, especially when she is given a mission. This mission can come as a vision, a dream, or a sign.

Sometimes, she is thrown into a mission without prior knowledge, because it's a learning experience. You might say that a certain part of your memory could go, *poof*, because divine connections need to happen through things that cannot be explained. Because we are not meant to know. The idea is that you need to intentionally forget something for the greater good, as there are connections that need to occur on other people's timelines that intersect with yours. For example, if you hadn't taken the ride to the amusement park, you wouldn't have helped a person from a burning car or stopped a person from being kidnapped.

There are many lives weaving together that we see, but you cannot. It is our job to make those connections. You are not alone. You all have your own angels. You are here to learn lessons. These lessons are the reason why you have your soul contract, why you are here at this time. It is all written in the Akashic records; each of you has a unique contract.

Time in our divine angel realm moves quickly, allowing us to be present anywhere and everywhere, as needed. And remember, calling upon your helper angel is not a one-time deal. It is an ongoing partnership because we are your teachers, and you are our students. You can always seek our help. All you need to do is ask.

So, if you ever find yourself at a crossroads or need celestial assistance, do not hesitate to reach out. And, hey, even though we may warn you not to sit on that broken toilet seat, we will laugh at you and your mishap if you take a tumble. As I mentioned, we balance being lighthearted and serious whenever the situation demands it. This is also a reminder that you all have free will. You can accept our guidance or take your own.

There is a secrecy surrounding what will happen in the future that we cannot reveal to you. However, angels will send you guidance in the form of signs that you can understand. The kind of signs you receive will depend on what is coming for you. If you ask for a specific sign, then you will encounter it. For example, if you want to know whether your child has been accepted into their desired college, you may start to see the name of the city where the school is located, or the logo of the college sports team. These are just a few examples of the signs that may appear.

I want you to know we will never force you to do anything you do not want to do, which is why you have free will. However, we provide guidance based on our experience and knowledge. We can see things you cannot see in our realm, and our advice can help you make better decisions. Ultimately, the choice is always yours to seek our help.

By the way, if your child tells you they have an imaginary friend, ask specific questions to find out more. Ask for the imaginary friend's name and tell your child to ask the friend if they can recite the Lord's Prayer. I know it might sound strange, but being specific will help you determine if it's an angel or something else in disguise.

Trust your intuition on this. You can ask for a sign that only you will recognize as a message from your angels. Go ask your angels now. We are waiting!

CHAPTER 3

GROWING UP EMMA

Emma Moment: *Angel told me to meditate because this will keep me balanced. She said it would give me clarity. I now love meditating. It grounds me and gives me energy from the earth. I feel rejuvenated when I can escape with nature and put my feet in the grass or the water. I am clearer, ideas pop into my head, and I feel more connected to the earth. It helps to calm me down. Strange things always happen to me. Yet when I meditate, they make sense somehow.*

I started calling these reflections my "Emma Moments," inspired by one of my mother's favorite shows growing up, Clarissa Explains It All. Clarissa would stop whatever she was doing and speak directly to the camera, sharing her thoughts. I thought it was so cool that I began doing it myself, pausing to narrate my life, even if no one else could hear me. These moments gave me a sense of control and comfort, especially when my world became unpredictable. There are many things that have happened to me, as you will see. However, one incident changed me forever because it awakened my gift of seeing. I suddenly knew things before they happened. Sit for a bit and let me tell you my story.

"I'm going to meditate at the park across the street," ten-year-old Emma declared. Her mom nodded.

Butterflies and bees drifted about the sky as they flew from flower to flower. When Emma rounded the corner, she saw her favorite tree standing tall in the small park across from her home. She plopped cross-legged onto the grass, feeling its softness against her skin. She closed her eyes and took three full, deep breaths, allowing the peace of nature to fill her until she heard nothing and was starting to drift to a higher realm.

Mickey, the German Shepherd K9, watched as Emma's neighbor, David, unlocked the garage and began taking out a lawnmower to cut the grass.

Something supernatural opened the gate, setting Mickey free. A voice whispered, "Go. stay with Emma."

Mickey's ears perked up, and he ran past the figure who opened the gate, following her direction. The gate closed quietly behind him. In the air, Mickey caught the familiar scent of the treats Emma always carried, peppermint and cinnamon mixed with irresistible sweetness. It was a fragrance that always drew him to her, and today, it lured him across the street to the park where she sat, his paws quickening with each step.

The golden sunlight bathed Emma in its comforting warmth, and then, suddenly, a bark echoed. Emma turned her head toward the sound, opening her eyes.

"Mickey!" she called out calmly as he ran up to her.

Animals were drawn to Emma in some natural, mysterious way.

Without flinching, she asked him if he had finished barking. When Mickey quieted, Emma offered him a treat if he behaved until she finished, and the canine crept over to her side. As promised, Emma gave him the snack as a reward for obeying her simple request. He settled beside her, and Emma returned to her meditation until she eventually dozed off into a peaceful dream lying on the grass. Mickey was sitting by her side as she drifted off to sleep.

Emma could see a young woman dressed in a flowy white gown that seemed to shimmer with an ethereal glow. She had an oval-shaped face with soft, warm brown eyes that held a depth of wisdom and kindness. Her long brown hair, with gentle waves, fell past her elbows, framing her delicate features.

She was Angel.

Angel's presence exuded the bright energy of a divine being of pure grace. Her skin had a subtle luminescence, enhancing her otherworldly aura, and her gentle smile conveyed both comfort and reassurance. Her gown moved gracefully with her as if it were woven from threads of light, and her overall demeanor radiated a sense of peace and benevolence.

"Good morning, Emma," Angel said.

Emma looked at her kindly before surprising her with an embrace. "Oh, Angel, I am so glad to see you again! It has been so long since we last spoke."

A gentle smile spread across Angel's face. "Yes, it has been too long," she replied. "Are you ready to talk about what's coming?"

Emma nodded as they began walking side-by-side into the mist. "I can't wait to hear all about it."

Mary bustled around the kitchen, tidying up after breakfast. "Elizabeth!" she called out, stacking up the used dishes and glasses in the sink. But her daughter Liz had been in her own world, playing video games.

Something on the counter caught her eye: a small white feather. A feather would always appear when there was a message about Emma. As she picked up the feather, a strange voice inside her head said, "Call for Emma."

Startled by the thought, Mary hesitated before calling out, "Emma! Could you come here, please?"

Liz yelled back to her from where she was playing video games, a birthday present from her father. "Why do you want her? She said she was going to the park after breakfast, and you said yes."

Mary remembered that she had had a conversation with Emma earlier, during which Emma had asked her for permission to go to the park. While the white feather made her pause, she didn't worry much about the park because it was a peaceful neighborhood and nothing bad had ever happened there. So, Mary went back to cleaning the kitchen.

As the man was about to put his key in the engine to start the car, a dark mist appeared out of nowhere and entered his body through his mouth. The man's eyes widened with excitement as the ominous entity surveyed the park, searching for the perfect spot. His prey was an unsuspecting young girl lying on the ground.

His heart raced as he took a deep breath and studied his prey. No adults were nearby to help her. The edges of his mouth lifted just enough to reveal a hint of malice; here was a gleam of satisfaction dancing in his eyes. He pulled a white handkerchief from his pocket, letting the contents drip from the bottle onto the car floor beneath him.

Without hesitation, he closed his car door with a loud creak and strode toward the park and the sleeping girl, picking up speed with each step until he was almost sprinting. Sweat beaded across his forehead as his gaze darted back and forth, his heart racing. He was so close now. With just a few more steps, the girl would be within reach.

Emma's spirit and Angel were locked in a deep conversation when Angel touched her shoulder, cutting Emma off mid-sentence. In a stern, commanding voice, she said, "It's time to wake up now."

As Emma stirred from her sleep, she opened her eyes and found herself a bit disoriented. At the sight of a stranger staring at her, fear spread throughout her body like ice water. Hadn't Mickey been there? She couldn't see him around.

The stranger was wearing an oversized black T-shirt, too-big blue jeans, and a red baseball hat. Emma noticed a skull tattoo on his left arm and a scar across his right cheek. But what scared her the most was the dark mist that surrounded his silhouette. She looked into his eyes, and they were completely black.

Before she could move, he reached for her, his lips twisted into a menacing smirk. His voice was low and threatening as he said, "Wake up, little girl." The man leaned closer. "Are you okay?" he asked, his tone low and menacing.

Emma could feel his icy-cold energy even before he could touch her, and she rolled away and stood, retreating back a step, then another.

He started to reach for her...

"What are you doing? And who are you?" she demanded.

The man mumbled something unintelligible, hastily trying to cover his face by pulling his red baseball hat down low.

Emma sensed the danger and saw an evil, dark entity again. A mist surrounded him as his eyes turned black before flickering back to normal. The sight of his malevolent eyes sent a shiver down her spine. She could see the black aura enveloping him and the evil energy emanating from him.

Little did she know that Mickey had gone from tree to tree, lifting his leg, marking his territory. He stepped out from behind a big tree, paused for a heartbeat, and suddenly barked and growled aggressively as though he sensed the danger.

"You better not touch me, or he will get you!" Emma threatened the bad guy.

Startled, the man stepped back. But the evil within him sprang forward again, and he grabbed her wrist, and she could not pull herself free.

Emma let out a piercing scream, making him jump in fear. He lunged forward, struggling to hold on to her to put the handkerchief over her mouth to silence her. Mickey charged, closing the barking distance, growling, and he launched into the man and bit his leg, refusing to let go.

In the kitchen, Mary wiped down the counter that still smelled of freshly cut lemons from making lemonade. Beside her, Liz reached out, attempting to steady a glass on the table with one hand while gathering up the silverware with the other. She had barely wrapped her fingers around its base when it slipped from her grasp, and the room was filled with the deafening sound of breaking glass, which shook Mary to her core.

Her knowing kicked in as she felt a sudden tightness in her chest, and a voice inside her head shouted, "Get Emma now!" Just then, from a distance, Mary heard Emma's piercing scream, one that sent chills down her spine.

Mary sprinted out of the room, shouting for Liz to stay put and call the police as she rushed to help Emma. Liz obeyed her, using the phone as she looked out the living room window, her eyes fixed on the events unfolding across the street in the park.

"911, what is your emergency?" the dispatcher's voice crackled through the line.

"I need the police right away! My sister, Emma, is in trouble in Front Street Park," Liz said urgently, her voice unwavering despite the chaos outside. She felt a surge of responsibility as she relayed every detail to the dispatcher, describing the suspicious man attempting to grab Emma and Emma's struggles to break free.

In the park, Liz spotted Mickey. As she watched, she couldn't contain her excitement. "Oh, wow! The K9 dog from our neighborhood just bit the guy!" Liz exclaimed into the phone to the dispatcher. "Please! Send someone quick!"

David had been eagerly waiting for spring to arrive, and the refreshing aroma of freshly cut grass was a sure sign that it had finally come. Lost in thought, he stepped out of his house, breathing in deeply, savoring the scent.

Suddenly, a high-pitched scream pierced the air, jolting David out of his daydream. He looked up and saw a man grabbing a young girl across the street in the park. As he scanned the scene, his dog Mickey darted across the grass toward the man. David blinked in surprise; Mickey had somehow managed to get out and was now racing to help the child.

David's heart raced as he sprinted toward the scene. As he ran, he saw Mickey pushing the man to the ground. He had to get the guy!

Mary's heart raced at the piercing scream that kept coming. She rushed out of her house and across the street toward the park where Emma was being attacked. Ahead of her, she sees her neighbor David race to the park toward his growling dog and a strange man.

As Mary got closer, she heard Emma's sobbing, and she ran faster.

David reached the man before her, subdued him, hand-cuffed him, before calling off Mickey, and holding the man as he heard a siren in the distance.

Mary ran up to Emma, who clung to her, and Mary could feel her body shaking as she passed her hand over her back, trying to calm her down, but her own heart was pounding as she hugged her child.

David turned toward Emma, who was crying into her mother's shoulder.

"It's okay, sweetie. *Mami* is here for you," Mary whispered, her heart breaking at Emma's sobs. She wiped away her own tears, the panic of hearing her daughter scream still fresh in her mind. She looked at David. "My other daughter called 911."

David nodded, and they exchanged a look. His knowing. Her relief.

"Can you tell me what happened?" she asked, her voice gentle but insistent.

Emma took a deep breath. "Mom, I was meditating in the park, lying here in the grass, when I opened my eyes and saw this man towering over me. His eyes were awful. Evil. I got so scared when he tried to touch me," Emma said with a shiver.

"I'm so sorry, Emma. That must have been terrifying," Mary said, holding her daughter's hand.

Emma continued, "Mickey was there with me, but I couldn't see him. The man's eyes turned completely black. That's when Mickey came running and bit him. He wouldn't let him go."

Mary nodded. "Mickey is a good dog; he knew something was wrong." Mary looked at David, then said, "I'm so glad Mickey was there to protect you."

David watched Mary and Emma, and then the police arrived on the scene. Two officers and another car were pulling up.

"I'm NYPD," David identified himself. "And this is my K9 dog, Mickey. We've apprehended the suspect who was trying to harm Emma here," he reported. The officers asked David a few questions, which he answered, and then went to speak with Mary and Emma.

As David stood there, he thought about what could have happened. He did not realize he had been so distracted cutting the grass that he had not noticed that Mickey was gone.

It was then that David realized something remarkable, as he watched Emma interact with Mickey, who was now sitting at her side. Mickey was at her side, not his. While he knew Mickey had a natural fondness for Emma, he had never fully grasped the depth of their connection until now. Mickey protected Emma. David often noticed how Emma would play with Mickey whenever he was off duty.

Despite the chaos, David felt a sense of pride. Both he and Mickey. They had acted quickly and saved a little girl's life. As he reflected on the event, not for the first time, he knew that he would always be grateful for Mickey's bravery and loyalty.

As Mary clasped her daughter in her arms, she noticed something glimmering in the sunlight amidst her daughter's long hair, a small white feather like the other one she had seen in her kitchen.

Emma leaned over to pat Mickey on his head and offered treats from her pocket to reward him for saving her. Mickey took the treat and jumped up at Emma happily.

Mary looked into David's eyes. "Thank you...Thank you. I don't know what—" she choked on her words as she profusely tried to thank him for rescuing her daughter, wiping the tears from her face with the back of her hand.

David smiled and said, "I'm just happy we were both able to help."

Mary reached out, touched the feather, and brushed away a lock of her daughter's hair from her face. A sense of relief filled her. Divine intervention had protected her daughter today. She now understood the sign of the feather.

That night, Mary reflected on Emma's ordeal. In her mind's eye, she relived the fear in her daughter's eyes and resolved to act. "I'm going to enroll the girls in self-defense classes," Mary decided aloud, determined to empower them with skills to protect themselves.

On a rainy afternoon, a few days later, the skies had cast a gray veil over the neighborhood. Inside Mary's cozy kitchen, however, it was warm and bright. The aroma of brewing tea and simmering herbs filled the air as Mary, her mom, and her sister Fatima sat around the kitchen island. Emma and Liz were at the table, drawing and chatting quietly.

Fatima and her mother, Ariana, exchanged glances. Then Ariana cleared her throat. "Emma, Liz," she said. "Come over here. We're going to start your lessons."

Curious, the girls put aside their drawings and walked over to the island where their Grandma Ariana reached into her bag and pulled out a book with a worn leather cover. It was titled *El Libro De Magia Paz*. The title was embossed in silver, and the book seemed to radiate an aura of something old.

Liz's eyes widened as she sat on a stool next to Emma. "What's that book, Grandma?"

"This," Ariana said, holding the book, "is *El Libro De Magia Paz*. It's a book of ancient recipes."

Emma, intrigued, asked, "What are we going to do with it?"

Tía Fatima took over, her voice steady and reassuring. "Today, we're going to start by making a sage cleansing bath. It's a simple but powerful ritual to cleanse and refresh your energy."

Ariana opened the book to a page about the sage cleansing bath, showing a list of ingredients and recipe instructions. She then reached into it and pulled out a small bag of sage. She placed it on the kitchen island beside the book.

"Liz, please get me a deep pot, pour some water into it, and set it on the stove." *Tía* Fatima instructed, then added, "*Gracias.*"

Liz did what she was told, taking a pot from the oven and placing it in the kitchen sink. She turned on the faucet and filled it halfway, then set it on the stove.

Tía Fatima explained to the girls about the uses of sage. She went over to the stove and carefully placed the pieces of sage into the pot, continuing to talk about the cleansing properties of the herb. The rain tapped softly against the windowpanes, providing a soothing backdrop to their lesson.

Emma Moment: *"Oh, for your information," Emma said with a laugh, "you might find it funny that we're taking the pot out of the oven, but that's where all Latina families put it. Where else would you store it? Under the sink? Definitely not!"*

"Grandma, what is the sage used for?" Emma asked.

Ariana smiled and explained, "Sage can be used for many things. It has many properties to ward off evil and calm the surrounding area, including your body."

"What do you mean, including your body, Grandma?" Liz inquired.

"You can use sage in three different ways," Ariana replied. "Take out your notepads and write this down.

"Here we go. One way to use sage is to boil it for a bath. Two, you can use sage to clean the floors of your home. Third, you can use sage to remove the evil influence surrounding you." Emma and Liz scribbled down notes as *Tía* Fatima continued to explain the benefits of sage. They didn't want to miss anything, and they could refer to their notes when they needed to.

"There is a lot of evil in the world, but we should not be afraid of it," she said. "We are protected by the benevolent light of the one source, or, as some say, God. When you are in a positive place, all good things come your way. But when there are obstacles at your crossroads, you can take a sage bath to cleanse and remove them."

As the water on the stove came to a boil, Mary turned it off. "Mom," Mary said to Ariana, "the water is done."

"Ok, *mi hija*," Ariana replied. "Take a strainer and pour the water into two bowls, one for Emma and the other for Liz."

Mary strained the water, which had a honey-colored hue to it.

The girls each took their bowls and added three drops of Florida water and holy water into them, as instructed. Then they lit a white candle for the bath. They passed the candle over each bowl for light and clarity, then poured cold water into the bowls to prevent burning their hands.

"Next, you say I am taking this sage bath to remove all bad influences from my path and body," Ariana explained. "I am attracting good energy toward me, or whatever comes to your mind, *chiquita*."

The girls placed their hands into the bowls and moved the water clockwise, repeating their intentions. They could feel the vibration of the bath. "Wow," they both said aloud.

Tía Fatima, Ariana, and Mary looked at each other, knowing this first lesson was successful. Ariana told the girls that they could take a sage bath whenever they felt out of balance, and *Tía* Fatima added that it was best to do it in the late afternoon and to stay indoors afterward. "You should not go out after a cleansing bath to avoid picking up any negative energies," Fatima advised.

"Remember," Mary said to both of them, "to repeat the intentions as you pour the sage water over your head."

The girls returned thirty minutes later, fresh and clean, with a white aura surrounding them both. Emma told them, "Wow! I feel so good after doing that. It's like something was repelled."

Liz agreed. "I feel it, too."

"Very good," Ariana said to her granddaughter. "Now let's learn how to make another bath, this one with mint, cinnamon, cloves, your favorite perfume, honey, holy water, Florida water, and a white candle."

Fatima agreed. "These ingredients are perfect for a rejuvenating bath."

Mary said, "Girls, you will both love the bath. It's a great way to relax after a long day."

Emma leaned forward, eyes wide with interest, and asked, "What is the bath for?"

Liz, always ready to share her knowledge, interrupted, "It's a good luck bath."

Mary's brow creased as she brought a hand to her mouth. With a questioning look, she asked Liz, "How do you know that?"

Liz responded, "I saw the words 'good luck' flash in my mind's eye."

Emma was still not convinced and asked for more details.

Mary explained, "The ingredients we have chosen are traditionally used to attract good luck and positive energy. The white candle represents purity, while the honey symbolizes sweetness and abundance. The Florida water is a powerful spiritual cleanser, and the mint, cinnamon, and cloves are known for their calming and healing properties. Adding holy water ties everything together."

As the girls listened, they could sense the excitement in the room as they prepared to make this good luck bath. The sound of laughter and chatter filled the air as they gathered the ingredients and began mixing them, guided by the knowledge of *Tía* Fatima and Ariana.

"Very good," Ariana told Liz.

Emma whispered, "Show off."

Liz stuck her tongue out at Emma.

Mary eyed them both and said, "None of that. We all should be respectful to one another."

"*Entiende*," Mary told Emma.

"Sorry," Emma said.

As the rain continued to fall outside, the women and girls spent the rest of the afternoon learning about sage kits that included selenite crystals and more, about good luck baths, and enjoying the warmth and comfort of the magical kitchen and their family of women.

One Sunday morning, they sat together in the church pews, listening to the sermon. Suddenly, Emma leaned over to Liz and whispered, "An older man is singing, and the music is getting louder."

As the congregation stood, Emma noticed an elderly man singing the 'Hallelujah Chorus' louder and louder. She covered her mouth and leaned toward him, her voice a hushed whisper.

"Excuse me," she said quietly. "Could you please stop singing? I cannot hear the sermon."

The man turned to her, and Emma froze. His presence seemed almost ethereal, his form glowing faintly with an other-worldly aura. He smiled gently as though he recognized her.

"Please tell my wife I'm okay," he said, his voice kind and calm. "She's been mourning my passing, and I want her to know I'm alright."

Emma's heart raced. She nodded, trying to keep her face neutral. She covered her mouth, concealing the fact that she was speaking during mass. "What's your name?" she asked, her voice barely a whisper.

"Byron Acevedo," he replied. "And my wife is Anna. She's sitting a few pews down with the black headpiece on."

Emma nodded and tried to keep a straight face as the sermon continued. Suddenly, the priest paused and announced, "Attention, everyone. The religious classes are starting now. All children, please make your way downstairs to the basement."

Emma and Liz noticed that Anna was also going downstairs to the basement for the religious classes. Emma held Liz's hand for support as they went down the stairs, watching for Anna.

As they reached the bottom of the stairs, Emma spotted Anna a few feet away. "Excuse me," she said. "You are Anna?"

Anna looked up. "Yes, that's me."

Emma took a deep breath and said, "I have a message for you from your husband, Byron."

Anna's eyes widened with surprise. "Byron?" she repeated.

Emma nodded, "He said tell her I am doing well,' he had said. "And whenever she thinks of me, I will be there for her."

Anna's face softened, and she said, "Thank you so much for telling me. I thought I felt his presence last night, as the lights kept flickering off and on."

Byron appeared next to Anna, his face breaking into a broad smile. Emma felt a sense of peace and connection, knowing that Byron was there for Anna and that she could give her the message.

Liz squeezed Emma's hand for support, realizing that Emma was tense. "Byron, please stop singing so loudly," Liz said. "We don't want to get in trouble with our parents for talking during mass."

Byron chuckled, and Anna and Emma smiled. As Byron

promised not to sing so loudly during mass again, Emma and Liz left for their classes, feeling a sense of comfort and connection that they had healed a widow's heart, but told the spirit to chill.

The neighborhood had awakened to a cooler, sunny day. No more gray rain, and the blue sky was clear. A gentle breeze blew through the trees, rustling the newly sprouted leaves and causing the cherry blossom petals to dance through the air. The birds sang merrily, flitting from branch to branch, and in the distance, children could be heard laughing and playing in the late afternoon.

Liz and Emma liked playing hide-and-seek in the park with their best friends, Emily Wu and Alina Montoya.

With her delicate features, pale skin, and a bouncing black ponytail, Emily had charm and expressive eyes, which were lit up with joy as she played with Emma. She wore a bright yellow tee and blue jean shorts, and she accidentally matched with Emma, who wore a yellow tee adorned with sunflowers and blue bicycle shorts. The two friends looked like a sunny pair against the park's green backdrop.

As they were hiding, Emma spotted a stray cat. "Look, Emily," she whispered. "That cat is coming toward us."

The cat, white with a distinctive black spot on its back in the shape of a heart, approached them and purred as they hid behind a huge tree. Emily turned to look, and as she held out her hand, the cat jumped into her arms, still purring contentedly.

Meanwhile, Liz was playing with Alina. Alina, who had

blonde hair that she had pulled back into a ponytail to keep cool, was wearing a pink summer dress. Liz, dressed in a blue jean jumper, emerged from her hiding spot just as Alina found the others. They all stood up together.

"You guys are it!" exclaimed Liz with a grin as she joined them.

When the afternoon was over and the sun began to set, they walked home as the sky turned a soft shade of pink and orange, casting a beautiful glow on the world around them.

"Wow, what a beautiful day it is," said Emma.

"I know! I could stay outside all day," agreed Liz.

As they were standing there, they noticed Emily rubbing her hand as if something were bothering her.

"What's the matter, Emily?" asked Alina.

"Nothing is wrong," Emily replied as she bent down. "I'm just putting down the cat."

When they looked back to where the cat had been, they realized it had vanished.

"Did you see where the cat went?" asked Emma.

"See what cat?" replied Liz and Alina in unison.

"A white cat with a black spot in the shape of a heart," Emily described.

But Alina and Liz just looked at them in confusion.

"I think you guys have been out in the sun for too long," teased Alina with a chuckle.

Only Emma and Emily exchanged a look of surprise. They could see the cat, while Liz and Alina could not. They shared the same gift of sight, and this realization deepened their connection.

"You know, Emily, I've never met anyone else who sees the same things I do, like people who have passed," Emma said quietly, her voice filled with a mix of curiosity, secrecy, and connection. "Until today, I thought I was the only one who could see them.

"I know what you mean," replied Emily. "It is finally nice to have someone to talk to outside my family."

"I agree with you," said Emma. "We have our own secret sight."

From that day forward, Emily and Emma's friendship blossomed as they discovered their shared ability to see things others couldn't. They spent hours sharing tales of ghostly cats, singing old men, and other phenomenon and mysterious sights that only they could perceive. Their bond grew stronger through these shared experiences, as they realized they weren't alone in their unique abilities. Their friendship became a source of comfort and understanding.

Chapter 4

Breaking Up

After two years of dating, Emma believed that Ben Jones was the man she would spend her life with. They shared their dreams and aspirations, talking about their future with unwavering certainty. Ben had seamlessly integrated into Emma's family, and she had become an integral part of his. They spoke often about marriage and starting a family, envisioning a lifetime of happiness together.

At the beginning of summer, Ben had become increasingly distant. He attributed it to his new real estate partnership, which brought in clients from New Jersey, Connecticut, Florida, and New York. Emma tried to be understanding despite feeling the strain of their lack of time together because of his frequent travel.

One evening, while watching TV, Ben randomly asked Emma who she thought would win the next basketball game. She answered without much thought, and the team she mentioned ended up winning. It didn't strike her as odd initially.

A few days later, when Ben texted her again about sports

predictions, Emma grew annoyed. "I don't know, Ben. Please, stop asking," she texted back. "We haven't spoken in three days, and all I get is a text about who will win?"

The following Friday, after another two weeks without seeing each other, Ben suggested they get together that night. Emma was thrilled to spend time with him and missed him. However, when she arrived at his place, he handed her a glass of wine and immediately turned on a soccer game between Real Madrid and Argentina.

As the game began, Ben was about to ask her who she thought would win, but Emma preemptively said, "I've got a headache, Ben. I really don't want to guess right now."

Emma began to suspect something wasn't right. Ben's behavior had shifted; he avoided meaningful conversations and seemed more interested in her predictions than in spending time together.

During the game, Ben casually mentioned that he had made a lot of money from his last bet, based on the team he had predicted would win. He kissed Emma on the cheek, but a sinking feeling settled in her stomach. It dawned on her that Ben might be using her to predict sports outcomes. Just that morning, he had texted her asking which NFL team would win between the San Francisco 49ers and the Kansas City Chiefs.

She answered without much thought, and the team she mentioned ended up winning. She didn't think much of it at the time.

Her phone rang, and she excused herself, seeking a moment of privacy; she went into his office.

"Hello," she said.

"Good evening, Ms. Duque. My name is Dale, and I'm from Crystals & Things. I'm sorry for the late call, but I received your order and wanted to correct an error I caught before placing it."

Emma's eyes fell upon a whiteboard with columns, each bearing the name of Ben and his two friends.

Dale continued, "Did you mean to order two hundred sage kits? As I know from your previous orders, you tend to order one hundred."

Emma noticed there were numbers written in each column under Ted and Arnold, which caught her attention: twenty, thirty, and Ben's name had fifty.

"Oh my god, Dale. Thank you so much for contacting me. It should be only one hundred in total," Emma told him.

"I will make the changes, and sorry for the late call. This will be shipped out tomorrow morning," Dale said.

"Thank you, and goodnight," Emma said.

"Good night, Ms. Duque."

As Emma walked closer to examine the whiteboard, a vision swept over her, a chilling scene unfolding in vivid detail.

In Ben's apartment living room, she saw Ben, Arnold, and Ted gathered around a poker table, their faces illuminated by flickering lights. Empty beer bottles and scattered poker chips added to the grimy atmosphere. Ben leaned in, a smile on his face, as he proposed the pact.

"We'll have sex with all the women we want," he declared, his voice dripping with arrogance. "And the first one to reach fifty gets the money."

Emma watched in horror as Arnold and Ted eagerly agreed, their eyes gleaming with anticipation. The three men sealed the deal with enthusiastic high-fives, their laughter echoing through the room. Ben pulled out a marker, wrote all three names, and drew a line on the whiteboard. He would have a line for each woman they would sleep with.

The scene shifted abruptly, and Emma was in a hotel room. She saw Ben with a strange woman, their bodies entwined in a moment of betrayal. She felt a cold shiver run down her spine as she watched the scene unfold, unable to look away. The woman's face was a blur, but Ben's expression was painfully apparent as he kissed her neck. His gaze was heavy with lust, and though there was a brief flicker of guilt in his eyes, it quickly disappeared, overpowered by the intensity of the moment.

The vision returned back to Ben and his friends around the table. Ben's voice was jubilant and gleeful. "I win," he declared, his words cutting through the silence like a knife.

"I just bedded number fifty earlier this morning." He held up a wad of cash, his eyes gleaming with victory as Arnold and Ted looked disappointed.

Emma stood frozen, the truth of the vision pressing down on her. She had seen the pact, the betrayal, the callousness of their actions. This was no mere figment of her imagination. It was a betrayal. She knew it with every fiber of her being, felt it in the depths of her soul. The truth was undeniable, and it left her reeling, praying desperately that she was wrong.

The reality was even crueler than she could have imagined. Ben had been using her all this time, exploiting her psychic abilities to make bets and get money, while she remained naive and blind to his cheating. With tears welling in her eyes, she confronted Ben, clutching the whiteboard.

"Emma, please, you've got it all wrong," Ben pleaded, his voice tinged with desperation. "Those numbers, they're not what you think. It's not what you're imagining."

Emma's breath caught in her throat as she turned to face

him, her eyes searching his for any hint of sincerity. "Then what are they, Ben? How do you explain this?"

Taking a step closer, Ben reached out to touch her trembling hand, his gaze pleading for understanding.

"It's not what you think, I promise. Those numbers are their sales from the homes sold. The guys and I are realtors, Emma. It was a bet of who could outsell the others, and that's all it is."

Emma's heart hammered in her chest as she struggled to comprehend his words. *Could it be true?* she wondered, her mind reeling with the possibility. She wanted to believe she had misinterpreted the vision and twisted it into something it was not. But as his words hung in the air between them, her face drained of color. Her eyes narrowed with the sharp realization that he was LYING: bold-faced and deliberate.

The truth came out, and Emma knew it. She had seen it with her own eyes, felt it in her soul, the knowing. This was no mere misunderstanding.

"I don't believe you," Emma whispered, barely taking a breath as she pulled away from his touch, and cried.

"I am psychic, Ben, and I know what I saw in my vision. I know the truth."

As Ben watched her gather her things, his expression was one of deep regret, because it was clear he knew he had lost her. No amount of explanations could undo the damage, the trust he had shattered through his own doing.

Emma took her things, her movements deliberate and final.

"Goodbye," she said, her voice cold and resolute, before she slammed the door, leaving Ben in silence.

After confronting Ben and breaking up with him, she made a vow to herself that she would never let anyone use her again for her gifts. As an adult, Emma had learned from past experiences. When she was younger, she had shared her psychic abilities with boyfriends who used her insights to win bets on sports games. They only sought her out during games, never valuing her beyond her gift. Emma felt used. They were interested in her gift, not her as a person. Proud of her abilities, she stopped disclosing them to men she dated. With Ben, she opened herself up again to trust. She never mentioned being intuitive to him with the hopes he would be different, that he loved her for who she was, not for what her gifts could provide. She had been foolishly trusting, blind to the truth until now.

With a sigh, Emma vowed to keep her guard up, determined to protect her heart from further pain. Deep down, a glimmer of hope remained beneath the layers of doubt and fear.

CHAPTER 5

EMMA

Emma flipped on the radio, and the Spice Girls' "Wannabe" filled the air, flooding her bedroom with infectious energy on this sunny Saturday afternoon. Sunlight streamed through the window blinds, casting playful patterns on the floor.

The room was a vibrant mix of her personality with soft pink walls. A Minnie Mouse clock hung above a small dresser adorned with various trinkets, including a collection of crystals and a rose-scented candle. A photograph of a third eye, intricately decorated with rhinestones, added a mystical touch to one wall. At the same time, a cherished picture of her family rested on the nightstand beside her full-size bed. The bed was dressed in a damask-patterned blanket, a pink Minnie Mouse pillow completing the theme. A cozy white faux fur throw blanket was draped casually over the foot of the bed, and a few well-loved books lay stacked on a small shelf, adding a whimsical charm to the space.

Grabbing a hairbrush as her impromptu microphone, she sang along at full volume, her wavy brown and ombre blond tips swirling around her face as she headbanged to the beat in the bright living room. Emma twirled in front of her long-length mirror, and sang away without a care in the world.

"Oh yes! Love this song!" she exclaimed.

She slipped on her jeans and a top, listening to La Mega 97.9 FM as "*La Gozadera*" by Gente De Zona. She shimmied around the room and swayed to the beat as she put on her socks and shoes.

Emma stood in front of the mirror again, adjusting the black T-shirt with bold white letters proclaiming, "My Body, My Choice." It wasn't just an outfit; it was her belief, her fight. After smoothing out her shirt, she grabbed her phone and texted Emily:

Emma: Hey! Want to help me collect canned goods for Our Lady of Sorrows in Corona? 😊

A few seconds later, her phone buzzed with Emily's reply.

Emily: Sure! 👍 But only if we can double it and donate to St. Michael's Roman Catholic Church in Flushing, too. 😉

Emma grinned at the screen and quickly typed back.

Emma: You got it! 🤍👍

Her friends often said she wore her heart on her sleeve, especially when it came to standing up for others. But they all knew Emma wasn't one to back down when something was wrong, especially when it came to women's rights. Her temper, something she attributed to her Latinx roots, flared brightest when injustice reared its ugly head.

Like last month, when her friend Sofia tried to sell her home in Briarwood, the realtor had quoted a price well below the market value. Emma arranged for a Caucasian friend to stand in during the next evaluation, and, unsurprisingly, the estimate jumped by thousands. Emma immediately confronted the real estate company. She was armed with video evidence and market comps, threatening to expose their discrimination to the media if they didn't correct it. The company had backed down quickly. This wasn't just talking. This was Emma fighting for what was right.

As the music played, Emma lifted her *bandera* and waved it in the air, yelling, "This is such a great track!" as she made her way to the living room. She increased the volume and began shaking her hips in time with the beat. Emma loved music and dancing, and it showed in her moves.

Her sister Liz emerged from the bathroom in her camouflage pajama dress, her short, shoulder-length hair bouncing with each step. Like Emma, Liz had light brown eyes and a curvy body. She grabbed the hairbrush from Emma's hand, and with a playful grin, she danced energetically to the infectious beats of "*La Gozadera*" that filled the room.

Their movements, fluid and energized, blended reggaeton's groove with the spirit of salsa and merengue. Liz cranked up the volume even higher, the music filling their cozy apartment. "We Duque sisters know how to move!" Liz laughed, twirling around and pulling Emma into their dance. Their laughter and the pulsing rhythm of the music filled the air, their joy and closeness evident in every step.

Sunlight streamed through the windows of their cozy apartment in Jackson Heights, and the warm rays illuminated their movements. As they twirled and leaped, their shadows danced along the walls.

Emma and Liz twirled around, catching their breath as the song reached a crescendo. Liz grinned at Emma and headed toward the kitchen.

A few moments later, Liz returned from the kitchen with a

steaming cup of coffee. She settled into her favorite spot on the couch, taking a sip and savoring the warmth. Across the room, Emma had switched the music to "Good Day" by Forrest Frank, her current favorite song. She sang along softly, lost in the uplifting melody.

After a thoughtful moment, Liz turned to Emma, a playful sparkle in her eyes. "I can't believe I'm getting married in twelve months!" she exclaimed between sips of coffee. "And the engagement party is next week. Already."

Emma smiled warmly, nodding in agreement. "Of course. I would never forget your party."

"I found my dress, and mom is working on booking the venue we all saw and loved."

Emma glanced at her sister. "That's a good beginning."

"We still need to order the cake, book the photographer, and the videographer. We just started on the guest list and chose the flowers, but the list should be dwindling down as we cross things off."

"That's great," Emma said. "I'm sure it's going to be a beautiful wedding."

Liz nodded. "I can't wait. And the best part is I'll have two weeks off from work for the honeymoon!"

"Getting two weeks? That's great! You both really deserve some time to relax and enjoy your new life together," Emma said.

Liz chuckled. "I know, I've been working hard for the past few years and deserve a break. I've saved up my vacation days for this occasion.

Emma agreed. "You do. Do you know where you're going yet?"

Liz's face lit up as she replied, "We finally decided on

Hawaii! We've always dreamed of visiting the island and its landmarks, and now we finally have the chance to do it."

"That sounds amazing. I'm so happy for you, Liz," she said.

Liz took another sip of her coffee and leaned back in her chair, looking out the window.

"Thanks, Emma. I'm emotional, but it's been a lot to plan. Mom has been a huge help, though. She's been busy running around and ensuring everything is perfect for the wedding. I don't know what we would do without her."

"Mom is a huge help," Emma agreed.

"At least things have been calm around the station," Liz said.

"You still love being a cop," Emma said. It was more of an observance than a question. "Your choice always surprised me."

Liz replied, "I made the decision so young. Do you remember that day when you were almost abducted in the park?"

Emma's mind went back to a memory from their childhood. The moment was etched in their memories forever. "Yes, I remember."

Liz took a deep breath. "That day changed everything for me. I knew I had to do something to make a difference and protect people. That's why I became a cop. Seeing David and Mickey stop that guy was heroic, and I wanted to be like them."

Emma looked at her sister with admiration. 'I'm so proud of you, Liz.'"

Her family felt the same way, too. Liz had recently applied to join the police K9 unit and was waiting for a spot to open.

"Angel warned me," Emma admitted for the first time. She warned me that an evil darkness would try to harm me, but she also promised that I would be protected because I was with the light."

Liz's jaw dropped in awe as Emma continued, "And then, Angel told me she opened the gate and let Mickey out to come to help me.

"That's incredible," Liz said. "You never told me that before."

"I know," Emma said.

Liz suddenly remembered something from her own past. "Wait, now that you mention it, I remember seeing Angel once when we were younger," she said. "We had a tea party, and she gave you a cup and then handed another cup to me. I think you were five, and I was four. You called her Angel. I remember she smiled at me and was so pretty. After that, I could not see her anymore, but I knew when she was around. I felt it."

As she spoke, the air seemed to shift, and just then, the soft buzz of an incoming FaceTime call interrupted her thoughts. Mary FaceTimed Liz at that moment.

"*Mi hija, ¿Cómo estás?*"

"Good, *Mami. Aqui* talking with Emma."

"Turn the phone so I can see Emma."

"*Hola, Mami,*" Emma said as she stuck her head in the phone frame.

"Liz, I wanted to let you know all is confirmed for the venue. *Tu Papa* cannot wait to have his father-daughter dance. He has been practicing with me." Mary laughed. "What were you talking about when you answered the phone? I heard you say, 'Angel'?"

"I was talking about that time when we were younger, and Angel gave me a cup."

Mary was silent as she remembered that day when her daughters were having a tea party with their toys.

"Hey, Mom? You still there?" Liz asked.

"Sorry, *niñas*. I remember that day. I was mopping the floors and passed your room. I saw not one but two cups flying in midair, and both of you grabbed them. Well, I was in shock, thinking it was a new gift. But then I heard both of you say, 'Thank you, Angel."

It still gave Mary goosebumps to this day as she recalled the memory, which even at the time she knew was good. She was able to sense it with her knowing.

A bright expression lit up Emma's features. "See? You know what I am talking about, then. Wow, *Mami*. You never told us you knew back then."

"Yeah, Mom," Liz agreed.

Mary laughed, "Girls, so many things have happened over the years that I could write a book."

Emma laughed, and Luz rolled her eyes.

"Well, I just wanted to let you know the good news about the venue, but I have to go now. I have another dancing session with your dad, and I want to get lucky." Mary smiled, then winked.

"Ugh! *Ay, Mami*! too much information!" Both girls said before hanging up.

Liz turned to Emma, "I hope that Gary and I will be like them when we are their age."

"You can if you want to make it work. *Tu sabes* that Mami and Papi made a lot of compromises, and I believe that is what kept them together. Oh, and their love for each other," Emma said.

"That is so true. I was going to say something before *Mami's* call. I just remembered."

Liz told Emma, "I have another story. Do you remember that day in the church when you asked me if I saw the old man singing, and I shook my head?"

As Liz finished recounting the story, they both erupted in giggles.

"I mean, can you believe it?" Liz said, still laughing. "I told that spirit to chill as if I could actually see him!"

Emma giggled. "There's never a dull moment with us, is there?"

"Duh," Liz replied. "I remember hearing the story of Anita Paz over the years, but it didn't really hit me until that day after the incident with David and Mickey."

Emma looked at her sister curiously. "What do you mean?"

"Well," Liz began, "we were both sitting down and talking about her story for the millionth time. And it really struck a chord with me because we heard the story many times, but we now had these gifts."

"I remember feeling like something had changed after that day."

They both sat in silence, lost in thought, reminiscing about the church story, their first paranormal experience.

She couldn't seem to shake her love for TV shows from the 90s and 2000s.

One of her favorites was *Clarissa Explains It All*, a hit TV show from back in the day. Her mom had introduced her to it, and Emma was hooked. She loved the way Clarissa would stop to talk to the camera. Just like Deadpool. Emma thought it was so cool that she started doing the same thing in her everyday life, calling these moments her "Emma Moments."

CHAPTER 6

RYAN

In the dimness of his bedroom, just past 5:30 a.m., Ryan Garcia sighed softly, pulling the blue plaid covers tighter around him. The room was bathed in a faint, early morning glow, seeping through the curtains, casting soft shadows across the walls adorned with framed medical certificates and a few motivational posters. A small nightstand with a lamp and a family picture frame stood beside his bed. In it, a smiling woman with kind eyes, his mother, Luna, and a younger girl with a mischievous grin, his sister, Mia, beamed back at him. Their presence brought a bittersweet comfort to the room, a reminder of love and loss that lingered in the air.

A sense of solitude weighed heavily upon Ryan as he lay there, his thoughts consumed by a yearning for companionship and the elusive prospect of building a life with someone special.

After completing his residency, Ryan had moved back to New York, lured by a prestigious orthopedic position at the Hospital for Special Surgery. However, his return was bittersweet, coinciding with the unraveling of his relationship with Isabella Carter. She had been offered a position in labor and delivery at Cedars-Sinai Medical Center in California, where her family lived. When Isabella broke the news to him, Ryan's heart sank. He realized their dreams were pulling them in different directions. Despite his efforts to find a compromise, they concluded that their paths were separating, and they parted ways.

It had been two years since the breakup, and although Ryan had tried dating, he found issues with every girl he met. His friend Mike had signed him up for speed dating. One girl, who was twenty-two years old, talked about herself for the entire five minutes. Another woman, who was twenty-five, kept repeating, "OMG! You're a doctor."

Ryan grappled with the reality of their separation, disappointment, longing, and a tinge of resentment swirled within him. Yet, beneath it all, there was a quiet understanding. Isabella's decision was her determination to pursue her own dreams. Though the pain of their parting lingered, Ryan couldn't help but feel a glimmer of hope stirring within him, opening himself up to unexpected opportunities and the possibility of still finding love.

Just last week, he attended a friend's wedding, where he witnessed an older couple dancing, their love and joy evident in every step. It reminded him that love could come at any stage in life, often when it was least expected. The memory of that couple stayed with him. Little did he know this newfound hope would soon lead to a chance meeting with someone who could change everything.

Alone in the darkness, though, Ryan found himself speaking aloud, a whispered plea to the mother who passed away, "Mom, when will I find someone to share my life with? Someone to create the kind of family you had?"

The silence was the only response his empty room offered.

It was Tuesday evening, 6 p.m., and Ryan was in the locker room with Mike and Harry at the YMCA West Side. Ryan laughed as Mike turned to Harry and said, "What's up, *Gringo*?" It was a playful nickname Mike always used for Harry.

Coincidentally sharing the same name as Prince Harry of England, he stood at the same height as the prince and had his red hair and twinkling blue eyes. His athletic build was evident under his YMCA jersey. Always ready with a joke or word of encouragement, Harry had a sarcastic wit akin to Chandler Bing from *Friends*, which often earned him teasing from Mike, who called him "*Gringo*." Harry was married to Beth and had a daughter, Kyra, who was four years old, and a son, Brandon, who had just turned ten.

Mike, resembling Judd Nelson from *The Breakfast Club* with his long hair, now in a man bun, had a charismatic presence. Half-Black and half-Dominican, he had a military officer's discipline from being in the Marine reserve and a voice that could sound like a drill sergeant when needed. Mike loved hiking, biking, and traveling, just as Sarah, his wife, did. He proudly wore a "girl dad" tee, reflecting his recent joy in being a father to his newborn, Mila.

Turning to Harry, Ryan asked, "Hey, Harry, did Beth see the doctor I recommended?"

Harry nodded, his easygoing demeanor evident as he replied, "Yes, she did. And I forgot to thank you. Beth loves Dr. Foster; she's thorough, thoughtful, and answers all my wife's questions."

"Happy she likes her," Ryan said, genuinely pleased.

Mike then turned to Harry, asking, "Hey, you are going on vacation this Friday?"

"Yup," Harry replied with a grin. "We're heading to Disney World. I got everything set up. The kids can't stop talking about it."

Turning to Ryan, Harry teased, "Hey, Ryan, you finally taking a vacation for Mia's wedding?"

"Who, Mr. Garcia, is going on vacation?" Mike asked sarcastically.

As Ryan quickly passed his hand over his hair, he replied, "Yes, starting on Thursday of next week, I'll be on vacation for a week."

After their brief conversation in the locker room, Ryan, Harry, and Mike quickly changed into their basketball gear. Mike pulled off his "girl dad" tee, revealing his well-defined body underneath, and threw on his YMCA jersey. Harry slipped on his basketball shoes with ease, while Ryan double-checked his shoelaces, a habit he had before every game.

As they made their way to the court, Mike nudged Harry with a playful slap on the back. "Hey, you ready to get schooled today?"

Harry rolled his eyes. "You wish."

Ryan chuckled, shaking his head at their friendly rivalry. "Come on, guys. Let's see who's got the skills today."

They entered the court, the sounds of bouncing basketballs and distant shouts filling the air as they began to play.

Standing tall with a warm complexion and a toned body after hours of workouts, Ryan exuded a quiet confidence that commanded attention. His brown hair, tousled from the exertion of the game, framed his handsome face, and he had striking hazel eyes that sparkled with determination.

Mike, Harry, and Ryan became more invested as the game heated up, their movements intense. In a moment of victory, Ryan took his shirt off, revealing his glistening chest and defined abs. Nearby, a group of women passing by couldn't help but steal glances, their attention momentarily diverted by the sight of his athletic form.

As one of the women in the gym walked past Ryan, she stumbled over her feet, blushing furiously. Her gaze lingered on Ryan's body for a moment, leaving her momentarily breathless, before she quickly regained her composure. Though her thoughts remained a mystery, her attraction was clear to anyone who happened to be watching.

Ryan made a well-placed shot. "You two talk a big game, but let's see if you can back it up."

Harry managed to outmaneuver Mike with a slick move and score a point. "That's how it's done!" he exclaimed, pumping his fist in the air.

Mike laughed, shaking his head. "Alright, alright, nice shot. But don't get too cocky. We've still got plenty of game left."

Not one to be outdone, Ryan seized his opportunity and made an impressive shot, earning cheers from the spectators on the sidelines. "In your face, Harry!" he shouted triumphantly.

Harry grinned, unfazed. "Let's see if you can keep it up."

Mike, Harry, and Ryan wrapped up their warm-up game just as the other players filtered onto the court, ready to start the game. The lanky referee blew the whistle, signaling the official start of the basketball game.

Mike dribbled the ball down the court with precision, passing it to Harry, who made a slick move to the left before sending it back to Mike. Mike caught it with one hand and, facing off against his defender, made a quick fake shot to the right. As the defender reacted, Mike swooped around and effortlessly laid up the ball, watching it sail through the hoop.

"Yeah, that's what I'm talking about!" Mike shouted as he watched the ball drop through the net.

The opposing team, fired up by the display, ramped up their intensity. Ryan responded with a series of powerful dunks, his confidence building with each slam.

Harry took his turn next, weaving through defenders and sinking a smooth shot. Mike followed up with a three-pointer.

Ryan's focus never wavered. His eyes locked on the hoop as he charged forward, leaping with explosive power. He released the ball with a satisfying snap, the net whispering with each successful shot. The small crowd watching the energy surged energetically with every basket, making the game feel like an electrifying battle of skill.

The sound of laughter and good-natured ribbing echoed across the court as all the players sprinted back and forth, sweat glistening on their faces. Each team was giving it their all, fueled by the unbreakable bond that had been formed over the last two years of playing together.

Amidst the intensity, their friendship showed through in small gestures: a pat on the back after a good play, shared jokes during breaks, and high-fives.

As the scoreboard lit up with them leading, it became evident that this game meant more to these friends than the competition. It was a celebration of their shared history, a testament to their enduring friendship. Beyond the points scored and the plays made, each moment on the court reaffirmed their joy in simply being together, united by their love for the game and each other.

After the game, Ryan, Mike, and Harry headed to the locker room to shower and change before their post-game ritual: grabbing food at the nearby diner. Ryan turned as he saw a locker door close, glancing over at Mike with a smile. Mike had tied his hair back before starting to get dressed in his black shorts and white tee.

"Hey, Mike, how's everything been with Mila and Sarah? Any new adventures in 'Girl Dad' territory?"

Mike's face lit up, a proud grin spreading across his face. "Oh man, you won't believe it. Mila turned three months old last week. She's growing so fast, and let me tell you, being a 'Girl Dad' is something else. She's already got me wrapped around her tiny finger."

Ryan's laughter was light and sincere. "I can imagine. How's Sarah handling everything?"

Mike gave a small smile, his expression softening. "Sarah's been amazing, you know. It's a lot of work, but she's been a rock."

Turning toward Harry, he asked, "Are you all ready for your trip?"

Harry smiled broadly. "Almost. I cannot wait to soak up every moment with the family. Time flies, man. Before I knew it, my daughter Brenda was starting pre-kindergarten, and my son Brandon was going into fifth grade in September."

"That's good, bruh," Ryan said to Harry.

The clock ticked past 8 p.m. as they left and walked up the bustling street toward Brooklyn Diner. Cars zipped by, their headlights casting fleeting shadows on the pavement. The diner's neon sign glowed warmly against the night sky, beckoning them in with promises of hearty comfort food and familiar surroundings.

Pushing open the diner door, they were greeted by the familiar aroma of freshly brewed coffee and the enticing sizzle of burgers on the grill, bringing back memories of countless meals shared over the years. The air was alive with the chatter of regulars and the low hum of a TV in the corner, broadcasting the evening news with a weather report. With their retro charm, the yellow vinyl booths gave the place a cozy, familial feel, a place where memories were made over shared meals and late-night conversations.

Seated in their favorite corner booth, Ryan smiled and gestured around. "This place," he said, "is the perfect mix of old-school charm and no-frills comfort. Remember that time we were here after that wild storm?"

Harry agreed, smiling as he gave a quick nod.

"Yeah, and Brooklyn gave us free pie because we were stuck here for hours."

Mike chuckled, adjusting his cap.

"It's like our second home, man. Always good for a post-workout refuel and some solid hangout time."

A waitress with a warm smile approached their table, menus in hand. "Hey, fellas, what can I get you tonight? Coffee, sandwiches, or maybe a slice of pie?"

They all ordered. The waitress nodded, scribbling down their orders with a practiced hand. "Got it. I'll be right back, gentlemen."

As she walked away, Ryan looked around with a thoughtful expression. The diner buzzed with the comforting sounds of clinking dishes and quiet conversations. He appreciated the familiar surroundings.

"Hey, Ryan," Harry began, his tone gentle but firm. "We've been noticing something lately, and we think it's time to discuss it."

Mike wiped the sweat from his forehead and leaned in.

"Dude, what's up with your love life? You've been out of the game for a while now."

Ryan rolled his eyes and shook his head. "I've been busy, man. Work's been wild."

Harry said, "We get it, but you can't neglect your personal life.

Ryan sighed. "I know, I know. But I want to be successful. I want to have my own practice someday."

Mike nodded. "Sure, but it's not all about work. You need to find happiness and companionship, too, bruh. How did that speed-dating event go last week? Did any sparks fly with any of the single ladies?"

Ryan chuckled lightly, stirring his water with a straw. "It was interesting. Met a few women, but nothing too exciting. One was constantly on her phone, and another wouldn't stop talking about herself. Oh, and here is the kicker: the last one just kept repeating, 'OMG, you're a doctor.' Seems like speed dating isn't my thing." Ryan shrugged. "I just haven't met the right woman yet."

Mike's face lit up. "Well, don't worry, buddy. Sarah has a single friend. Maybe we can set you up on a blind date."

Ryan raised an eyebrow, amused but slightly apprehensive. "I appreciate the thought, but I'm unsure if blind dates are worth it."

Harry nudged him playfully. "Come on, Ryan. You never know until you try. Plus, Mike and I can vet her first to make sure she's not a serial killer."

Mike looked at him with a smile and said, "I think we need to get you out of your shell. You used to be quite the ladies' man, remember?"

Ryan laughed and shook his head. "That was a long time ago, Mike."

Harry said, "Yeah, and we can't forget that time we hit the club, and you were the center of attention. Didn't you see the crowd at the Y today? They weren't looking at us."

Ryan blushed, "Alright, alright, I get it. You want me to get back out there and stop being so stubborn."

Their food arrived, served hot and steaming. Harry and Mike dug into their burgers while Ryan thoughtfully took one-half of his turkey sandwich, his mind lingering on their earlier conversation.

After a few bites, Mike leaned back, noticing Ryan was lost in deep thought. "How are you really doing?"

Ryan sighed, running a hand through his hair. "It's been a bit of a struggle, to be honest. I've been so focused on work and haven't had time for much else. Living at my uncle's place hasn't been the best. I just wanted to stay there at first to keep an eye on my little cousin." Ryan often found himself preoccupied with thoughts of his cousin's health, trying to keep his worries to himself.

"I haven't had time to even search for a place to live."

Harry looked at Ryan with empathy. "I get it. It's tough, especially with your job."

Mike chimed in, "But hey, you've got us. And we're always here to help you navigate the city and help you find your own place."

Ryan smiled gratefully, "Thanks, guys. I appreciate it. You know, growing up without my dad and losing my mom to cancer made me cautious about change. It often feels like when I let someone in, they don't stay for long."

Harry looked at his group of friends, his expression sympathetic. "I understand, Ryan. But, sometimes, change is good."

Mike added thoughtfully, "And remember, Ryan, love isn't about perfection or figuring everything out. It's about being willing to let someone in, flaws and all. You must break down those walls you've built up and allow yourself to take risks. Well, maybe it's time to start paying attention. You never know who you might meet."

Mike agreed with a nod. "Exactly. It's about taking small steps, allowing yourself to adjust and grow."

Ryan listened intently, the words sinking in.. He felt a pang of resistance, unsure if he was ready to change. Yet, as he pondered their words, he began to see the wisdom in their advice. True success wasn't just about chasing goals, but also about nurturing meaningful relationships and finding genuine happiness. It was a perspective shift he hadn't fully considered before. For the first time in a long while, he felt a glimmer of hope stirring within him. Just maybe it was time to take a chance on love and embrace the unknown. "Yeah, I guess I need to work on that, breaking down the walls I've built up."

Harry offered a reassuring smile. "And we're here, bro."

As their meal wrapped up, the trio settled their bill and stepped out of the diner, greeted by the evening moon. The bustling city streets buzzed with energy as they bid farewell on the sidewalk.

"Thanks for the great company, guys," Ryan said, a genuine smile lighting up his face. "Sorry about missing last week. I know with my job, getting called in at the last minute is a

bummer. But getting together is important to me. I need something outside the hospital."

Mike clapped him on the back. "Absolutely, Ryan. Just hit
me up anytime, bruh. We will make it happen. Take care.

Harry nodded. "For sure. See you next week, if you don't
end up on call and don't forget what we talked about, bro."

Grateful, Ryan thanked his friends and headed to catch his
train home.

CHAPTER 7

SISTERLY LOVE

Emma looked up as the door opened, and Liz walked in, with tears on her face. "What's wrong?"

Liz's voice trembled as she replied, "My K9 dog, Chewy, was not compatible with me and was reassigned to another officer."

Hearing the heartbreaking news, Emma's heart sank. She couldn't imagine what Liz felt after finally getting accepted into the unit. She put her laptop down, jumped from the sofa, ran over to Liz, and hugged her tightly.

Liz broke down in Emma's arms, tears streaming down her face.

Emma whispered soothingly, "I'm here for you, Liz. I'm so sorry this happened. We'll get through this together."

"I just couldn't make progress with Chewy, and my boss had Chewy train with someone else, and he took to him better than I."

Emma nodded, recalling how Liz had dedicated herself to Chewy's training day and night. "I know, Liz," Emma began softly, her voice filled with understanding. "You trained with him 24/7. I saw how much effort you put into every session, and you will get paired up with another dog. Sometimes dogs pick their handler, and this one was not the one."

Liz looked up at Emma, tears glistening in her eyes, grateful. "Thank you for being here, Emma. I don't know what I'd do without you."

Emma smiled and hugged Liz once more, her voice gentle. "That's what sisters are for. We'll get through this together."

Emma did her best to cheer her sister up. When she got home a few days later, she picked up Liz's favorite coffee ice cream and surprised her.

"Hey, sis, I got you a pint of your favorite coffee ice cream," Emma said, holding it out for her.

"Wow, you're the best. Thank you so much," Liz replied with a smile. They sat down and started enjoying the ice cream.

While they ate, a tear rolled down Emma's cheek. "It's hitting me that you'll be leaving soon, and we won't be having these chit-chats as frequently anymore."

Liz noticed the tear on Emma's face and said, "Don't worry, sis. We can still have our chit-chats and catch up, don't think I won't come to visit, okay?" Liz added with a playful grin, her tone light but firm. "I'll make time for you, *carajo*. We're family. Or do you think I will not come to visit?"

"Really? I didn't think I would see you as much since newlyweds love privacy!" Emma exclaimed, taking a tissue to dab her eye.

"Emma, we are *hermanas* and will always be there for each other," Liz said reassuringly.

"*Coño*," Liz said to Emma, making her smile, and soon they began giggling.

"Love you, sis," Emma said.

"Right back at you, sis," Liz replied as they hugged.

Emma glanced at her laptop on the coffee table. "Guess I need to get back to work," she said reluctantly.

Liz nodded, understanding. "Alright. I'll let you be. Thanks again for the ice cream."

Emma moved to her small wooden desk by the window, opening her laptop. The faint hum of the computer and the soft clicking of keys filled the room as she returned to managing her online business, Anita Inspires. The website sold incense kits, sage, tees, and more. She reviewed emails, processed orders, and replied to customer inquiries; her mind was occupied with the details of her work.

Liz came into the room a half hour later and sat back on the sofa before she asked, "How do you keep track of everything, Em?"

Emma smiled, a mixture of pride and determination in her eyes. "I have a spreadsheet where I put my information for all my sales and returns. My tax person loves my accounting system."

Liz's expression clearly showed she was impressed. "Sounds like you've got it all figured out."

Emma smiled, feeling a sense of accomplishment as she continued to navigate her tasks.

Notifications of new orders brought a sense of normalcy, grounding her amidst the busy afternoon. She felt blessed to be able to do what she loved and steadily grow her online business. All it took was a bit of organization and magic.

Three weeks later, they found themselves at Juniper Park on a beautiful sunny morning. Emma settled on the grass with a book while Liz wandered farther down to join her monthly yoga group for their practice.

While Emma was sitting alone under a tree, a soggy little bundle of fur jumped into her lap. A puppy. Startled, she looked up to find a woman with two German Shepherd puppies struggling to control them. The woman smiled at Emma, her gaze lingering on the puppy perched on Emma's lap, and asked, "Do you want him?"

Unable to form words, she nodded mutely and stared into the pup's eyes. She felt the same spark of love and loyalty that Mickey had lit inside of her so many years ago.

When the woman said, "He is all yours," Emma knew that fate had decided the pup would be Liz's. She talked to the lady about the dog's condition and his vet papers. The funny thing was that she had it all with her, since she was on her way to the pet adoption clinic, because they were too much for her to manage.

When Liz finished her yoga class at the park, she joined Emma.

"Look what jumped into my lap. A beautiful German Shepard puppy."

"But how?" Liz said.

"This is a gift from the divine and, eventually, your training partner. If you want him?"

Liz bent down, and the puppy jumped into her arms. He immediately started to lick her face. "Oh, yes, I want him."

"Well, that settles it then. He is now yours, and the lady gave me all the paperwork for him, too."

Emma Moment: *After my sister, Liz, lost her training partner, and*

The atmosphere buzzed with excitement as the clock struck six that Saturday evening. The wedding venue hall hummed with chatter and laughter, illuminated by the warm glow of twinkling fairy lights. Family members gathered, dressed in their finest attire, ready to celebrate the joyous occasion.

Mateo and Mary Duque stood proudly at the front of the room, dressed in a matching blue dress and suit, their faces beaming with pride as they addressed the crowd. "We would like to welcome you all to this special celebration," Mateo began. His salt-and-pepper hair added a distinguished touch to him; he looked like an older Andrés Garcia, a leading man from a Spanish *novela*. Despite his age, he maintained a healthy body, a testament to his daily walks. As he spoke, his voice carried a warmth that filled the room. "Tonight, we gather to announce the engagement of our beloved daughter, Elizabeth Duque, to her fiancé, Gary Walters."

Cheers erupted from the crowd as Liz and Gary stood hand in hand, their smiles radiant with happiness. Gary's parents, siblings, and grandparents stood beside him, sharing in the joy of the moment.

Meanwhile, Emma was mingling around the room when her cousin, Jasmin Duque, bumped into her.

"Hi, cuz," Jasmin said.

"What up, girl? How have you been, *prima*?" Emma said. They kissed each other's cheeks.

"Good, and you?" Jasmin asked.

"I cannot complain. Oh, great. Here comes your mom, I know she will ask that same question, *"Y el novio?* If I have a boyfriend."* Emma says, shaking her head.

"*Coño*, she is still doing that. *Ah, Dios Mio!*" she said, putting her hand on her head.

Emma did have her fair share of insecurities. However, the one that stood out the most was her single status. Family gatherings were always so brutal. Her family sarcastically called her *una solterona*, an old maid, when the answer was *no tengo novio* to their immediate inquisition on her dating status.

Sigh.

Aunt Esther was making her way over, a curious gleam in her eye.

"Isn't it wonderful that Liz is getting married?" Aunt Esther exclaimed, her excitement palpable.

Emma offered a warm smile in response, though she knew what was coming next. "Yes, it's truly a joyous occasion," she replied politely.

Aunt Esther's gaze turned probing as she leaned in closer. "And what about you, Emma? Are you seeing anyone special?" she asked, her tone tinged with concern.

Emma's smile did not falter as she shook her head. "No, not at the moment," she admitted.

Aunt Esther's expression grew serious as she took Emma's

hand in hers. "You don't want to be *vieja y sin pareja y solterona*," she warned. Old, single, and spinster.

Emma's response was swift. She took off her cardigan sweater, revealing her t-shirt with the bold statement emblazoned "*No Tengo Novio*." It meant, "I don't have a boyfriend." She met her aunt's gaze squarely, defiance flickering in her eyes.

Aunt Esther's cheeks flushed.

Jasmine piped up, "*Ah, Mami*, you need to stop. I'm also single, and you don't see anyone else asking me."

"I appreciate your concern, Aunt Esther, but I'm in no rush," Emma said firmly. "I'll date when I'm ready, so please stop asking me as if I am a lost cause."

Emma took a breath, steadying herself against the familiar sting of Aunt Esther's persistent inquiries into her personal life. "I know you mean well, but sometimes it feels like you're more curious than concerned," Emma admitted bluntly, her voice tinged with frustration. "There are days when I feel pressured like I'm supposed to fit into some timeline of when things should happen."

Aunt Esther nodded thoughtfully, her expression softening with realization. "I just want you to be happy, dear. But I understand now. I'll try not to pry."

Emma smiled gratefully, appreciating her aunt's willingness to understand. "Thank you. I'll let you know when there's something to share."

Jasmin put her arm around her mom and said, "*Mami*, leave Emma alone, and let's go see Auntie Ariana." As they left, Jasmin turned around and winked at her.

Emma smiled back and whispered, "Thank you, *prima*."

She was only twenty-five, not in her thirties. It was not like she wanted to get married soon. Maybe in the future, but right now, she wanted to experience as many things as possible while she was young.

She had thought her intuition was always spot-on. But then, there was Ben. As the sad memory faded, Emma's focus returned to her sister's engagement party. She wiped a tear from her eyes as she watched their happiness. Despite her argument, she was young and had time for a relationship she longed for love, for someone who would see her for who she truly was, not just for her gifts and how they could enrich themselves from them. She wanted to find true love. Maybe it was a wish that would soon come true. She just had to believe there was someone out there for her.

Emma felt a gentle hand on her shoulder as Ed Sheehan's heartfelt "Perfect" filled the hall. She turned to her father, Mateo, who was there with a soft smile.

"Come on, Emma," he said, his voice warm and inviting. "Let's show them how it's done."

"Yes, *Papi*, let's show them how it's done." As Mateo took her hand and led her to the dance floor, she could not help but feel a sense of comfort wash over her.

As they began to sway to the music, Mateo looked into Emma's eyes with a father's love. "You know, *mi hija*," he said softly, "you are perfect just as you are. Any man would be *loco* not to see that."

Emma felt a lump form in her throat as she absorbed her father's words. For so long, she had doubted herself and questioned her worth in the eyes of others. But at that moment, as she danced with her father, she realized that she was enough, just as she was. Her desire was simple yet profound: to find a man who would love her unconditionally, accepting her for who she was, not merely for her psychic gifts. Seeing her sister about to marry and witnessing her parents' relationship only intensified Emma's yearning for a meaningful connection, one based on genuine love and acceptance.

Meanwhile, as Mary watched from the sidelines, her heart filled with a mix of pride and nostalgia, seeing her daughter dancing with her father, Emma was on the cusp of something good happening. It was the knowing within Mary that told her so. As she continued watching them dance, she felt a sense of gratitude wash over her, accompanied by a deep-seated belief that unseen forces were working on something.

Chapter 8

Emma's Chance Trip

Emma Moment: *Have you ever stepped out of the house, only to realize you've forgotten something important? As you stand there, trying to remember, it's like the world has cast a spell of confusion over you, making it impossible to recall. But why does that happen?*

Emma dreamed she visited her parents. She stood before them in the living room, but they could not see her. Desperate, she waved her hands and called out to them, but they remained oblivious, as if she were invisible. The terror of being unseen jolted her awake, her body drenched in sweat. Shaking off the remnants of the dream, she reassured herself, repeating, "It was only a dream; it was only a dream."

As she lay there, the longing to see her parents grew stronger. It had been weeks since she had taken a break, and with the Fourth of July approaching, memories of past celebrations in East Meadow, Long Island, flooded her mind. It was Wednesday afternoon, so why not surprise them? The thought of reconnecting with her family, combined with the need for a change of scenery, propelled her to grab her phone and start punching in their number.

However, as her finger hovered over the call button, Emma hesitated. A mischievous grin spread across her face. Instead of calling, she decided she would surprise them in person. With renewed determination, she leaped out of bed and began packing her weekend bag.

She left a note to tell Liz where she was going since Liz spent last night at Gary's after her shift at work.

Emma moved about her apartment, gathering her bag, laptop, and a few clothes for the road. She grabbed the charger for her phone and keys and made the sign of the cross as she closed the door behind her. She navigated the bustling streets, entering her favorite La Nueva Bakery to grab a coffee on the go. She headed for the train.

Emma found a seat by the window next to the conductor. About fifteen minutes later, the train approached Penn Station. Emma stood up as the doors opened and weaved through the crowd of commuters. She needed to catch her connecting train to her parents' home in East Meadow, Long Island.

As Emma glanced at the board and saw that the Babylon train was leaving soon. Hurrying, she barely noticed the commotion around her. A man being chased by three police officers shoved her as he ran past. The impact sent her crashing into a metal support beam on the platform. Her head struck it hard enough to blur her vision. Her phone flew from her hand, its screen cracking on impact. She began to fall.

Her vision wavered, and everything felt too loud and too far away. She blinked hard, trying to pull herself back into focus. While two of the officers chasing the man quickly moved to secure the area and ensure the suspect was apprehended, the third knelt beside Emma. Seeing that she was disoriented, he pulled out his radio and called 911.

Paramedics arrived shortly after and assessed Emma's condition, noting the impact on her head. Gently, the paramedics placed her on the stretcher.

The ambulance doors closed with a solid *thud*, and the vehicle sped off toward NY Presbyterian Hospital. Inside, the paramedics continued to monitor Emma's vital signs, preparing for her arrival at the hospital.

At the hospital's emergency entrance, the medical team quickly took over her care. The bustling ER of NY Presbyterian Hospital was filled with activity. The reality of the situation was stark and sobering, contrasting sharply with the normalcy of her day just hours before. The beeping of monitors and the murmur of medical staff surrounded her.

Her ER doctor, a Filipino neurologist with a badge that read Dr. Oshiro, was calm and reassuring. His dark hair was neatly trimmed, and wire-rimmed glasses framed his face. He wore a crisp white coat over his green scrubs. His head nurse introduced herself as Betty. She was petite and had a fiery, spirited attitude that radiated from her Puerto Rican background. Her dark hair was pulled back into a tight bun, and her expressive eyes conveyed both empathy and determination. She wore blue scrubs and her energy and competence shined through as she worked. Dr. Oshiro and Nurse Betty moved a green curtain to provide some privacy. They took her vitals.

Dr. Oshiro gently touched Emma's back. "She has a noticeable bump where she was hit on the head. Schedule a CT. I want to make sure there is no internal bleeding. And get her an ice pack for the lump."

Nurse Betty acknowledged the instruction with a brisk nod and moved quickly to carry out the order.

Dr. Oshiro gave Emma a reassuring smile. "Try to relax. We'll take good care of you. We'll get you through this. Just hang in there while we check everything thoroughly."

A few minutes later, Betty returned and gave her a reassuring smile. "All set for the CT-Scan, Dr. Oshiro. I'll take her up myself." She placed the ice pack on the back of Emma's head.

Emma took a deep breath as she was wheeled out of the room toward the radiology area.

An hour later, Emma was in a hospital room after her CT scan was completed. The persistent ache in her head made it hard to focus, and the lights overhead did little to ease her discomfort. She turned to Nurse Betty, who had been monitoring her. "My head hurts."

Looking sympathetic but firm, Nurse Betty replied, "I'm sorry, Emma, but we can't give you any medication until we get the CT scan results back. I will give you another ice pack for your head."

Emma sighed in frustration, feeling the exhaustion and pain. She took the new ice pack and placed it back on her head. Night had fallen outside, and Dr. Oshiro had finished his shift, and Dr. Gloria Smith had taken over the night shift.

Dr. Smith entered the room with a reassuring smile. She wore a surgical cap with her black hair pulled back neatly, green scrubs, and black Crocs. Her bright green eyes conveyed both competence and empathy. "Good evening, Emma. I've got some news for you, both good and bad."

Emma looked up, her gaze wary but hopeful. "Give me the good news first."

"The CT scan showed no internal bleeding, which is good. I'm going to prescribe some pain medication to help with your headache. We had held off on giving you any medication for two reasons: first, we needed to determine if you might require surgery, and second, it took some time to locate your information in our system to confirm whether you had any allergies to medications, which we have now confirmed you do not."

Emma's face brightened slightly. "When can I leave?"

Dr. Smith's tone shifted. "Now for the bad news. The CT scan showed a mild traumatic brain injury, commonly known as a concussion, caused by the blow to your head. Some brain injuries can lead to cognitive changes, memory lapses, trouble with motor control, or difficulty recognizing familiar people or objects. Because of that, we have a protocol to keep you under observation for twenty-four hours to watch for delayed complications. It is better to be cautious."

Emma's face fell slightly. "So, what does this mean for me? Will I have ongoing issues?"

Dr. Smith gave a sympathetic nod. "You may or may not experience some memory issues or other symptoms related to the concussion. We will monitor you closely to make sure there are no complications. For now, you will need to stay here under observation."

She shivered slightly as she thought about how close she had come to a much more serious situation. "I guess I'll be staying here tonight. I do have one request. I'm starving. Can I get something to eat along with that pain medication?"

Dr. Smith chuckled softly. "Of course. Nurse Thalia, could you please arrange some food for Emma and get her the medication?"

"Sure thing, Dr. Smith," Nurse Thalia said.

Emma looked up at Dr. Smith and asked, "What time tomorrow will I be released?"

"That will depend on how you feel in the morning," Dr. Smith replied. "Dr. Oshiro will decide and discuss it with you when he comes in."

"Got it. Thank you, Dr. Smith," Emma said, her voice trailing off as she began to feel the effects of her medication.

Dr. Smith gave her a reassuring nod. "Good night, Emma." The doctor left, leaving Emma alone for a few minutes. Emma had the thought she should call Liz, but she didn't see her phone or other belongings.

The nurse returned shortly with a tray of food, adjusting the hospital bed table and placing it in front of Emma. "Here's your meal and the medication. The doctor said to take it with your food; it should help with your headache."

"Thank you so much," Emma said, her voice tinged with relief.

Nurse Thalia returned about thirty minutes later. "I see you've eaten. Good. I'm going to check your vitals now and let you get some rest," Nurse Thalia said gently. "The medication should be kicking in soon."

"Thank you," Emma murmured, her eyes closing. "Good night. I'm so tired, and my head is pounding."

Nurse Thalia smiled warmly. "The doctor's medication should help ease the pain. Get some sleep."

Emma's head drifted to the side, and she succumbed to the fatigue, falling into a deep, much-needed sleep.

Emma woke up Thursday morning to the beeping of monitors and the soft chat of the medical staff. Outside her room, she could hear bustling with activity down the hall. As Emma turned her head, she looked for the call remote, which was next to her, and she pressed the call button. Her head still throbbed painfully, and she felt the urgent need to use the bathroom. She hoped that she might be able to go home today.

Nurse Thalia popped her head in. "Good morning, Emma. What do you need?"

Emma looked up with a strained smile. "I need to use the bathroom, but my head is hurting. Could I have some more pain medication?"

Nurse Thalia nodded understandingly. "Of course. Let me help you to the bathroom, and then I'll get you your medication and breakfast."

Emma attempted to stand but felt a wave of dizziness and had to sit back down. "I need help."

Nurse Thalia helped her, then got her tucked back in bed. "I'll get you your breakfast and get you the pain medication. The new shift is coming in shortly, and Dr. Oshiro will check on you again soon."

The breakfast trays had just arrived, and the kitchen staff were placing them on each patient's bedside table. Emma took a deep breath, grateful for the smell of food and coffee. "Thank you," she said as Thalia handed her the pain medication.

As she ate, Emma thought that hospital food had really improved a lot. The scrambled eggs tasted surprisingly good.

"How are you feeling?" Nurse Thalia asked, clearing the tray.

"A bit better, but my head still hurts."

"The medicine should kick in soon," Thalia said gently.

"The doctor will be by shortly. I'll check on you again once you've had some rest."

Dr. Oshiro arrived shortly after, checked her chart, then gently touched the back of her head to assess the swelling. "The lump has gone down," he said. "I'll have another ice pack brought in, and I'm recommending a second CT scan just to be sure everything still looks good."

Emma nodded, feeling a mix of relief and apprehension. "How long will it take for the results?"

"About an hour or so," Dr. Oshiro replied. "I'll let you know as soon as we have them."

By noon, Emma had returned to her bed and had drifted off to sleep, waiting for Dr. Oshiro's update. She was half awake when she heard Dr. Oshiro in the hall outside her room.

"Hey, Ryan. We've had a few cases coming in, but it's not too busy yet."

The voices of the two men were muffled, and as they began walking down the hall, their conversation grew unclear. Too tired to focus, Emma turned over and let the soothing hum of the hospital drift her back to sleep.

"Emma, it's time to wake up."

Emma stirred and rubbed her eyes. Dr. Oshiro stood in front of the bed.

"Hey, Doc. I hope you've got good news for me."

"I do. Your scans are clear, so we're going to discharge you with a prescription for pain medication," Dr. Oshiro said.

"I'll probably grab the meds at the pharmacy here at the hospital. That'll be faster," Emma said.

"Keep using the cold pack on the bump and take it easy for the next couple of days. If you notice any memory lapses or feel off, don't panic. Just rest, breathe, and reach out if anything feels unusual."

He had her stand and walk a few steps to make sure she was steady. Emma moved slowly but with more strength now that she had eaten.

Satisfied, Dr. Oshiro handed her the discharge paperwork.

"Thank you for everything," Emma said before he left.

Emma gathered her backpack and overnight bag and headed to the bathroom to change. She stopped by the hospital pharmacy to pick up her prescription and left the hospital, feeling a mix of relief and exhaustion.

As she stepped outside into the bright, sunny afternoon, she pulled one of the handles off her backpack and opened the front pocket to check her phone. Tapping the screen, she saw that it did not turn on. Her phone was dead. She quickly pulled out her MetroCard, closed the front pocket, and put her backpack back on.

Standing on the corner of York Avenue and 68th Street, Emma tried to remember why she had gone to Penn Station in the first place. Her memory was hazy, just out of reach. Maybe going back there would help. She decided to walk up to Lexington Avenue and take the train to Penn Station, hoping the familiar sights might trigger something and help her piece it all together.

Emma descended the steps to the platform of the six train, the turnstile clattering as people walked in and out. She swiped her MetroCard and slipped through. Her gaze snapped toward the downtown train stairs as the rumble of the approaching train grew louder.

The train's brakes screeched, and the conductor's voice crackled over the intercom: "Stand clear of the closing doors, please."

She wove through the mass of passengers and squeezed into a seat near a graffiti-splattered ad for a technical school. She glanced at the banner advertisements for legal services and food delivery services plastered on the train, their bright colors momentarily catching her eye.

The subway map overhead seemed to sway as the train jolted forward. Flickering lights cast fleeting shadows on her face, and her mind, clouded and weary, struggled to connect the dots of her journey.

The loudspeaker announced, "42nd Street, Times Square." Emma gathered her things and maneuvered through the congested crowd to transfer to the next train that would go to Penn Station. The station buzzed with the frantic energy of rush hour as the train pulled in with a hiss.

The doors closed behind her as she squeezed into the packed car, her head throbbing in the press of bodies.

"Oh, why did I come here?" she muttered, frustration thick in her voice. The memory still refused to surface.

The loudspeaker crackled. "There is congestion up ahead, and we will be moving shortly."

"Oh, brother," grumbled a man on a bike, his messenger bag swaying with each impatient shift as he fidgeted on the train.

A nearby woman sighed, "Not again."

Emma glanced around, trying to anchor herself amidst the confusion. *Never a dull day,* she thought, though the words felt hollow.

The train lurched forward, only to halt abruptly. The conductor's voice resumed, "Due to a sick passenger in the train ahead of us, we are being held momentarily."

"*Coño!*" Emma said under her breath, frustration mingling with the murmurs of discontent around her.

The minutes dragged on, and the train remained stalled. It was now four thirty p.m., and Emma had been stuck for over an

hour. The chatter of irritated passengers filled the air, punctu-
ated by exclamations of frustration. "Whoever was sick should
have been taken off the train so we could move," one passenger
said, and others agreed aloud. Finally, the conductor announced
they would be leaving.

Emma let out a sigh of relief when the train finally rolled
into Penn Station. She stumbled out, her head still pounding.
The escalator to the platform was out of service, so she made
her way to the stairs and began to climb. A wave of dizziness hit
her halfway up. She gripped the handrail, trying to steady
herself.

At the top, the chaotic rush of commuters surged around
her. She pressed against the wall, overwhelmed by the sea of
people racing in every direction.

"Ma'am, are you feeling okay?" an officer asked, concern
etched on his face.

Emma forced a weak smile. "Just too many people. I need a
moment to catch my breath."

The officer's gaze lingered, skeptical but accepting. "All
right, ma'am, if you're sure. Have a good day."

She spotted a small table inside a nearby restaurant and sank
into the chair, trying to collect her thoughts. Her head
pounded, and the disorientation made her feel as if she were
floating in a fog.

She reached into her bag and pulled out a small bottle of
water she had taken from the hospital. Her hands trembled as
she fumbled with the medication. Panic surged through her,
and she closed her eyes, willing herself to remember. Everything
felt like a distant dream, slipping further away with each passing
moment.

Taking a deep breath, Emma tried to steady herself. Her

thoughts felt scattered, like puzzle pieces that would not quite fit together. Where was she going? Where was home?

She opened her wallet, hoping to find something to ground her. Her heart sank when she realized her ID was missing. "What the hell," she muttered, frustration rising in her throat. Her address was on that ID. She vaguely remembered the EMT saying the cop took her ID as they put her into the ambulance.

Emma pushed herself up from the table, her head still throbbing as the medication slowly took effect.

She found herself standing near the entrance to the LIRR trains and paused. The crowds, the movement, and the signs overwhelmed her. She rubbed her temple and closed her eyes, trying to tune it all out and center herself.

Once outside, the city noise swelled around her as she walked along 34th Street. She moved slowly, trying to stay calm despite the confusion pressing in. She stopped and looked around. Nothing felt familiar.

She turned back toward Penn Station, hoping to recognize something. Anxiety stirred in her chest as she whispered, "Where am I even going?" The question lingered in the air, unanswered, as she kept walking, searching for something familiar.

CHAPTER 9

RYAN'S FIRST GLIMPSE

"Dr. Garcia, your next patient is a thirteen-year-old girl with a possibly broken ankle in room four. Her X-ray is on the board," said Nurse Vanessa Andrews as she finished reading the chart. She took off her wire-rimmed glasses and handed the patient's chart to him. Her silver hair was pulled back, accentuating her grandmotherly face.

"Got it, Vanessa."

Dr. Ryan Garcia walked into the hospital's examination room. The room was adorned with cheerful paintings depicting vibrant scenes of New York City and a funky cat clock ticking softly on the wall. The air conditioning provided welcome relief from the hot and humid July weather outside, maintaining a comfortable atmosphere despite the summer heat. Inside waiting was thirteen-year-old patient and her mom.

"Hello, Ashley. I'm Dr. Garcia. I hear you have hurt your ankle."

Ashley said, "Yes. My left ankle hurts whenever I put weight on it. This happened yesterday after somersaulting in gymnastics. When I landed, I think I came down harder than I thought. Ever since yesterday, it hurts."

Ashley's mother added, "She wouldn't stop complaining that walking hurt. I thought she'd better have someone take a look at it."

Ryan turned on the X-ray board light and carefully examined the image. The fracture was clear. He pointed to the hairline fracture, then turned to Ashley and her mom. "You fractured it, young lady. You'll need a cast to keep your foot and ankle immobile while it heals," he said after switching off the light board. "You'll need to wear it for about six to eight weeks, and we'll have you come back and to monitor the healing process." He made some notes and handed the chart to Nurse Andrews.

Ashley realized her mom was staring at the doctor and said, "Wow, you're handsome. Do you have a girlfriend?"

Ryan chuckled and replied, "You're too young for me."

But then her mother interrupted in a sultry voice, "I'm not."

This made him cough, and he was not sure how to respond without it getting any more uncomfortable than it was.

Nurse Andrews said, "He is engaged."

Ryan gave her a knowing nod of thanks and explained that someone would be soon to take care of her cast. He started to leave, but Ashley's mother quickly stood up, blocking his exit.

"Thank you, Dr. Garcia." She shook his hand and slipped him her card. She added, "I'm a divorce attorney. That's my specialty."

Ryan just nodded and left.

Nurse Vanessa met him in the physicians' area outside the rear of the exam room.

Ryan said, "Thanks for stepping in. That was awkward. I don't know what to do when patients' mothers hit on me like that."

Nurse Vanessa chuckled. "No problem. I hope I can say that you are engaged, and mean it soon."

Ryan just shook his head and laughed.

"Patients' moms hitting on you is becoming a regular occurrence," Vanessa said, following him into his office.

"I just haven't found the right woman yet, and you are already taken," he joked.

"You've been single for a while now, and you work a lot. I know, since I've been a nurse for twenty-five years now, and new doctors always want to make their mark, but at the expense of their happiness. It wouldn't hurt to get out there and meet someone new."

Ryan looked at her and deflected again. "You let me know when you chuck that husband of yours out on his ear."

Vanessa laughed. "Well, I've kept him around for thirty-five years, so don't hold your breath."

"You're breaking my heart, Vanessa."

"I probably shouldn't tell you about all the bets the girls in the break room have placed on how long you can remain unattached."

Ryan raised an eyebrow, amused and slightly taken aback. "Is that so? I suppose I should feel flattered."

Before she walked away, Vanessa said, "Oh, I left you that test result you requested about your cousin Matthew on your desk."

Ryan glanced up and nodded. "Thanks." He approached his desk and picked up the folder, apprehensively to look at his cousin's test results. His eyes narrowed slightly as he scanned the documents, and his grip tightened on the contents. After a moment, he folded the results carefully and slid them into an envelope. He placed the envelope in his gym bag to give to Anne later.

Ryan turned to Vanessa and asked, "After the next patient in room three, will you manage the paperwork? He is the last patient before my vacation starts."

"Of course, Dr. Garcia. Enjoy your sister's wedding and tell her congratulations from me."

"Will do." Ryan said, feeling the tensions of his long day at work. He was looking forward to seeing his friends later at the Y to unwind and relax. However, his thoughts kept drifting back to the test results.

After finishing the last patient's chart, Ryan signed all the required paperwork on his desk, turned all the folders in, and put them on Vanessa's desk. A satisfied smile spread across his face as he prepared to officially start his vacation. He took off his white doctor's coat and tossed it in the laundry bag in his locker. With his gym bag slung over his shoulder, he was ready to head out and meet up with the guys for their usual basketball game. He took out his phone and quickly texted the group chat:

Ryan: Hey, guys, just wrapping up at the office. See you soon!

He hit send and waited for the elevator doors to open. Once inside, the doors slid shut, and the elevator began its descent. Ryan's phone buzzed with new messages.

Mike: We need to cancel tonight because the YMCA has booked the gym, and it's not available.

Harry: I was just about to text you both that Mila is sick, and it looks like Sarah is coming down with what she has. I won't be able to make it.

Ryan read the texts with a sigh, his excitement for the game deflated. He typed out a response as the elevator descended.

Ryan: I got it. Let me know what day is good, bro, and I'll be there. I hope Mila and Sarah feel better soon. TTYL.

The guys quickly replied.

Mike: Got it. I'll be there, bro.

Harry: Definitely. Catch up soon!

Ryan left the hospital and made his way across the street to NY Presbyterian Hospital. It was a quiet Wednesday afternoon at 12:45 p.m. The ER was bustling with activity but not yet overwhelming, as the day was still young. The sterile, bright lights of the ER illuminated the waiting area, reflecting off the white tiles and linoleum floors. The rhythmic beeping of monitors and the soft murmur of conversations filled the air, creating a backdrop of organized chaos.

Ryan spotted Justin Oshiro coming from one of the rooms, finishing up a set of vitals on a patient. As Ryan approached, he noticed that the patient was a woman.

Wow, she's stunning.

Justin looked up and smiled. "Hey, Ryan."

"Busy day?" Ryan asked, trying to mask his reaction to Justin's patient.

"It's not too crazy yet." Justin caught him staring at the woman. "That's Emma. She was brought in yesterday with a concussion from an incident on the subway, and we're just doing some final checks before her release."

Ryan looked over at Emma, noting her serene expression as she slept.

Justin continued, "What brings you by with that gym bag?"

"I was heading to the Y, but my game got canceled at the last minute. Are you working late today?"

"Actually, I'm about to finish my last rounds. The shift changes at 3:30, and I'm free after that. How about we go for a run and grab a bite to eat?"

Ryan, not wanting to head home just yet, agreed. "Sure, that sounds great. I'll change in the locker room and meet you in the staff lounge."

"Perfect," Justin said.

Ryan walked toward the staff locker room, where he quickly changed into his workout gear. The cool fabric of his workout clothes felt refreshing after his day in scrubs. Once he was ready, he made a right to the staff lounge.

The lounge was spacious and inviting, with newly updated sofas arranged in a cozy area. Soft, plush cushions and modern furniture created a comfortable atmosphere, perfect for unwinding after a long shift. The sunlight streaming through large windows cast a warm glow over the space. A few staff were scattered around, chatting or enjoying a break from their busy day.

Ryan crossed to a sofa near the window, sat down and set his gym bag down beside him.. As he waited for Justin to finish his rounds, he glanced around, appreciating the relaxed ambiance of the lounge. The hum of conversation and the occasional clink of coffee mugs created a tranquil contrast to the hectic ER.

Justin and Ryan left their gym bags in Justin's locker and decided to take a jog at Andrew Haswell Green Park.

"So, what's new with you?" Justin asked, glancing over his shoulder as they jogged.

"My friend Mike set me up on a speed dating event," Ryan replied, shaking his head.

"Let's just say I won't be doing that again."

"Why not?"

"The women were pretty self-absorbed, or only wanted to date a doctor, or couldn't put down their cell phone for ten minutes. I'm not going back," Ryan said with a laugh.

"Well, you're more than welcome to join me next weekend. I'm hitting up some lounges with a couple of friends here in the city. It'll be fun," Justin offered.

"You know what? I'll be there," Ryan agreed.

"Cool," Justin said, picking up speed. "Now, get moving slowpoke. The loser buys food," he said, racing ahead of Ryan.

"Slowpoke?" Ryan called out as he closed the distance between them.

"Race you to the park and back to the hospital. The loser buys food!" Justin shouted as Ryan caught up and was almost alongside.

"Now who is the slowpoke?" Ryan started to pass Justin. "You tried that when we were in medical school, and I beat you then. Looks like I'm passing you now!"

Justin exclaimed a curse as Ryan zoomed past him. They both laughed, the friendly competition energizing their run.

As they jogged down York Avenue, the cityscape whizzed by with neon signs, bustling shops, and the occasional street performer adding to the urban rhythm. When they reached the park, the open expanse of lush greenery was a refreshing contrast to the surrounding tall buildings, offering a sense of relief and tranquility. The sun dipped lower in the sky, casting long shadows as they made their way back.

After they returned to the locker room and changed into their streetwear. Justin suggested they grab a bite at Andrew's NYC Diner.

"I'm meeting some friends there who are going to the movies. Do you want to come?"

Ryan shook his head. "No, I'm going to try to head home and I need to get a gift for Mia's wedding this weekend."

They were still deep in conversation when they got off the train at Penn Station and walked toward the diner. They settled into a booth, where the clatter of dishes and hum of conversation created a comforting backdrop. The scent of sizzling bacon and brewing coffee enveloped them as they looked at the menus.

They ordered, and Ryan said, "You haven't lost your speed, old man."

"Nope," Justin replied with a grin. "I run every other day. Not like when we were roommates in medical school."

"I used to outrun you all the time." Ryan laughed.

"Not all the time. That's not how I remember it," Justin joked back. "Beginner's luck or something like that."

"Remember when we had that epic study session and ordered way too much pizza?" Ryan chuckled.

"Man, I couldn't eat pizza for a month, and I lived on pizza and ramen," Justin laughed.

"And remember that girl who had a thing for you? The one from our anatomy class?" Ryan asked.

"Yeah, I remember. Angie. We ended up together for a while after that," Justin said.

They both talked and laughed heartily through their food.

As they finished and waved to the waitress for the check, Ryan said, "I'll cover the bill, even though I won."

"Hey, go right ahead. You know you only got lucky."

Ryan paid the bill and left a tip, and they both walked out of the diner.

"It was good catching up with you," Ryan said.

"You too, bro. Don't be a stranger. Remember, I know where you work," Justin replied.

With a final wave over his shoulder, Ryan made his way toward Penn Station, and the familiar chaos of New York City enveloped him. It was 5 p.m. Yellow taxis honked and zoomed past. Delivery bikes wove through the throng of pedestrians. As he crossed the street, a yellow cab halted abruptly in front of him, nearly clipping his side.

"Watch how you're driving!" Ryan yelled, giving the cabbie the finger.

The driver, unfazed, sped off into the sea of traffic, another testament to the city's hectic pace. Several tourists stood in front of Madison Square Garden, snapping photos and chattering excitedly.

The towering buildings of Midtown cast long shadows as he passed, but the summer sun still managed to break through, bathing the cityscape in a golden light. He looked up and saw the iconic entrance to Penn Station looming ahead, a steady stream of commuters flowing in and out. The station's large glass doors reflected the city's hustle and bustle.

Ryan paused at the doors, searching his wallet for his MetroCard while commuters streamed out of the station.

CHAPTER 10

A MOMENT OF DESTINY

Emma spun around, hopelessly confused, and into a solid, towering male figure. She looked up. A tall, handsome man stood before her. She was in awe of his presence. A navy V-neck T-shirt hugged his body as if he were the god Thor himself. He also had the cutest hazel eyes she had ever seen.

"Hey." He reached out to steady her. "Are you okay?"

Emma winced, her head still throbbing and blinked up at him, trying to focus through the haze of pain. "Yeah," she managed, rubbing her temple. "I'm sorry. I wasn't watching where I was going. I have a bad headache, and everything's a little blurry. I'm not sure where I was going."

"Your vision is blurry? Are you confused? You should get checked out by a doctor." Ryan suggested.

"I did and was discharged from ER earlier this afternoon. Dr. Oshiro told me it was a concussion and to take it easy," Emma replied.

"I just left Justin. Dr. Oshiro. He's a friend. I went to med school with him. Justin, is good, and you should follow his instructions. Maybe you should sit down. Standing here isn't good if you are in pain." He looked around. "There is nowhere here to sit."

His gaze shifted as if he had sensed something. There was a long pause before he asked, "Can I help you get home?"

Emma looked at him. "I don't remember where home is," she admitted in a choked voice.

He stared at her for a long moment, as if he couldn't tear his gaze away. He seemed to pause in thought, then said, "Since you are not sure where you are going, do you want to come home with me? I don't live very far away.

Emma looked at Ryan, her head still throbbing with pain.

"I'm sorry. That came out wrong. You seem out of it. I was trying to help. I'm Ryan Garcia, a doctor." He pulled out a hospital ID with his name. "What is your name?" Ryan asked, his concern evident.

"Emma Duque," she said, fatigue in her voice as she hugged her bag to her chest almost defensively. She felt a mix of fear and confusion as she tried to decide what to do. The sun was setting, and it was getting late, and she was feeling weak and unsure.

A white feather floated down in front of her and landed on Ryan Garcia's shoulder.

Emma heard a soft, angelic whisper in her right ear telling her to say, "Yes." She couldn't ignore the supernatural significance of the moment. She knew that the feather was a sign and that the voice she heard was more than just a figment of her imagination. She trusted in the voice.

"Yes, I'll go with you."

Ryan took her arm gently, worried she might faint on him, and said, "We can take a taxi to my aunt and uncle's place in the Bronx. Given your headache and the train ride ahead, it might be better than dealing with the rush hour commute."

Emma winced as she touched the swollen spot on her head, nodding in agreement. "A taxi sounds like a good idea."

Ryan hailed a passing cab and helped her inside, ensuring she was comfortable before giving the driver his destination. As they pulled away from the curb, Ryan turned to Emma with a reassuring smile.

Ryan then quickly texted Uncle Theo and Aunt Anne that he was bringing home a woman who needed a place to spend the night. They had an arrangement; Ryan just needed to inform them of guests beforehand.

"I've texted my aunt and uncle that we're on our way," Ryan explained, his voice calm and reassuring. "They're expecting us. It is safe, Emma.

"Thank you." Emma turned her head to look at Ryan. She kept quiet for a bit, wanting to hide her uncertainty about where she was going. She was also trying to process why, in the world, she would agree to go home with a total stranger. Deep within her heart, though, she felt the need to heed and trust the voice. Emma sat in the back seat of the taxi, frowning at her phone.

Ryan, noticing her expression, turned his head in her direction and asked, "Everything okay?"

Emma looked up, surprised. "Oh, no, my phone is cracked," she said, holding the screen up.

"How did you crack your phone?" Ryan asked.

"I was pushed on the subway and injured my head, which is

why I was at the hospital seeing your friend, Dr. Oshiro. I remember dropping it when I hit the ground."

Ryan shook his head sympathetically. "Ah, that's frustrating," he said. "Did you notify your family about what happened?"

"No, I did not have a chance. I only just found my phone before I ran into you. It was in a pocket. I thought I had lost it between the subway, the ambulance ride, and the hospital," Emma said, her voice rising with frustration. "I have my battery charger with me, so I'll try to charge it when I get to your place, if it will work. My family must be worried," she admitted, looking a bit overwhelmed.

Ryan noticed her distress and smiled reassuringly. "Hey, would you like to use my phone to call them?"

Emma shook her head, looking a bit embarrassed. "I can't. I don't know their number by heart. With the phone, I just hit my contact."

"Don't worry," Ryan said, the corners of his eyes crinkling with confidence. "You can charge your phone when we get to my place and call your parents, let them know you're all right."

"Thanks. That sounds like a plan," Emma said, feeling a bit relieved.

The taxi moved along the highway, and as they passed by Yankee Stadium. Emma stared out the window, quietly lost in thought.

Yankee Stadium. I remember going there as a kid. It feels familiar, but nothing else is coming back to me.

The taxi stopped before a modest house near Co-op City, and she felt her heartbeat faster. An inexplicable force led her to this place. Emma felt an inner knowing guiding her, but what could the reason be?

Ryan asked the driver to wait as he hopped out of the taxi. He offered her his hand and helped Emma out of the cab.

"Hold a moment," he called back over his shoulder to the driver.

Ryan stopped and fumbled inside his athletic jacket pocket for his keys. As they walked up to the door, Emma thought she saw someone watching them from the corner of her eye, but when she turned, nothing was there. He put in the key and unlocked the door.

Ryan whipped around and told Emma to hang tight outside for a second. Then he went in to get the extra money for the taxi.

She said, "Ok." He walked inside while she waited for him to return at the door.

Suddenly, the door swung open, revealing an older woman with gray hair styled in a bun. She was dressed in a flowing floral dress, accessorized with a rosary around her neck. Her warm smile lit up her hazel eyes, which crinkled with kindness as she greeted them.

"We've been expecting you!" she exclaimed, looking in the direction Ryan went. She turned back to look at Emma.

Emma looked surprised and responded, "You have?"

"Yes! And do not forget to tell Ryan that I am proud of my *chichi*. He will know what that means."

With that, she shut the door again. Just then, Ryan hurried out and paid for the taxi. He turned and opened the door, telling Emma to go in.

She walked into the foyer of the house, greeted by the comforting sight of a mirror on the wall, reflecting the warm light from a vintage chandelier above. A small table by the entrance held neatly stacked mail and a delicate crystal vase filled with fresh flowers, their sweet fragrance permeating the air. The decor spoke of lived-in elegance, with tasteful accents hinting at cherished family memories.

Ryan guided Emma further into the house. The living room unfolded before them, a spacious yet cozy retreat from the bustling city outside. Sunlight filtered through cream-colored curtains with sunflowers, casting gentle patterns on the polished hardwood floors. A plush love seat and a large, overstuffed sofa dominated the room. The love seat, with its soft, inviting fabric, offered a comfortable spot to sink into, while the sofa, with its worn leather cushions, exuded a lived-in charm. Hand-knit throws added a cozy touch to a pair of armchairs in the sitting area. A bookshelf along one wall overflowed with a diverse collection of books, from hardcover to well-thumbed paperbacks. The opposite wall featured framed diplomas and certificates, marking academic achievements and professional milestones. A stack of record albums lined one of the shelves, adding a nostalgic touch to the room.

Emma took in the room's homey feeling and casual atmosphere. She glanced around, noticing the soft glow of a table lamp in the corner, casting a warm pool of light over a collection of framed photographs on a nearby side table. The cozy atmosphere of the living room made her feel a little more at ease as Ryan guided her further into the house.

A teenaged boy who looked about fifteen, sat on the sofa, surrounded by books and papers.

"What's up, Alex, my man?" Ryan asked.

Alex swung his curly brown hair out of his face and stood up. He wore a Marvel T-shirt and jeans without shoes. He grinned at them. "Not much, I'm just doing some homework from my summer classes."

Ryan gestured toward Emma. "I'd like you to meet Emma Duque. Emma, this is my cousin Alex."

Emma smiled and extended her hand to him. "Hi."

"Hi," Alex replied, shaking her hand. Then he turned around again, saying, "I have to get back to my homework if I am to have this paper done by tomorrow. I'll take it all to my room," he said, gathering up his books and papers. He paused. "It was nice meeting you, Emma."

As he left the living room, Ryan steered Emma toward the kitchen.

The door to the garage swung open, revealing Ryan's aunt, Anne, and his cousin, Alyssa, carrying grocery bags. Alyssa, a lively ten-year-old with a mischievous spark in her eyes, bounced into the room. She wore a "Be Kind" T-shirt, faded blue jeans, and bright sneakers. Her curly hair was tied back in a messy ponytail. She carried two grocery bags.

"Anna, Alyssa, this is Emma. Anna is my aunt, and Alyssa is my favorite cousin."

They laughed.

Anne looked at Emma and said, "Oh! Any friend of Ryan is welcome in our home. Have a seat."

"Thank you!" Her eyes lit up, and a flicker of relief swept over her, making her feel better. Anne's sunny attitude sent warmth flooding through Emma's chest.

Alyssa couldn't help but giggle.

Emma looked at Alyssa and asked, "What is so funny? Want to share?"

"Ryan has never brought a girl into the house before." Alyssa squealed. "I think you two like each other."

Ryan flushed.

Her comment made Emma blush.

Then Alyssa started singing, "Ryan and Emma sitting in a tree, K-I-S-S-I-N-G. First comes love, then comes marriage, and then comes—"

"Knock it off, squirt." Ryan gave her a quick hug, and her giggles returned as he tickled her. Laughter echoed throughout the house.

Anne quickly stepped forward. "We just got back from the grocery store," she said, hoping to change the subject. "Alyssa, you can start putting away the groceries.

"Sure," she replied.

"I'm going to put this away and get your room ready." Ryan picked up her bag and took it with him.

Emma smiled, feeling more at ease as she settled into the rhythm of the household.

"Can I help with anything?" she offered.

"Oh, sure!" Alyssa exclaimed, not waiting for Anne to respond, and handed her a bag of vegetables.

"You can put these in the last clear drawers on the bottom of the fridge."

Emma took the bag from Alyssa and headed over to the fridge, carefully opening the door and finding the designated drawers.

Anne took out a frying pan, poured a little olive oil, and turned on the stove.

Alyssa chattered away about all the fun events at summer school that day as she finished putting the food away with Emma. Anne declared that she was making her special chicken dish with a side of salad because she was watching her figure.

Alyssa rolled her eyes and said, "Oh, Mom, you always say that."

Emma glanced at Anne, acknowledging that she looked

great. She was slim and had curves in the right places. Emma kept her thoughts to herself, not wanting to vocalize what she thought for fear of saying something inappropriate.

Anne prepared dinner and asked Emma to occasionally help either to add seasoning to the chicken or help with the salad. Emma thought it was impossible to mess up a salad, given that all she had to do was clean the lettuce and add everything else to the salad bowl.

"Alyssa, please set the table for dinner and add an extra plate for our guest," Anne instructed her.

Alyssa rolled her eyes and scolded her mom, "You know Alex should help, too. This chore isn't just for women."

Emma could not help but laugh at Alyssa's remark. The girl's sharp wit amused her.

Anne chuckled softly, shaking her head. "You're right. Alex should help, too. But he has an important school paper. I'll let him know as soon as he gets out of his writing cave."

Alyssa's face flushed slightly, and she let out an exasperated sigh. She marched over to the kitchen cabinet and flung it open with a sharp motion. The plates and utensils clattered as she pulled them out with an impatient jerk. As Alyssa set the table, the clinks of the dishes were loud. Her frustration was evident in the way she slammed the utensils down, each action underscoring her annoyance.

Anne glanced over at Alyssa, shaking her head slightly, and ignored the drama queen moment and continued preparing the rest of the meal without letting Alyssa's display faze her.

Emma's mouth watered as the scent of chicken drifted into her nose, making her stomach grumble in hunger.

"Your stomach is talking. Here. Eat this till dinner is ready." Anne handed her a piece of Italian bread.

After she ate the bread, Emma took her phone and charger out of her bag and asked Anne, "Where can I charge my phone?"

"There's an outlet by the microwave," Anne replied.

"Thanks." Emma went to charge her phone but discovered after a few moments that it wouldn't turn on. With the cracked screen there was nothing.

"It's completely dead," she said, frustrated.

Ryan was heading out of the kitchen when he overheard the conversation. He offered Emma his phone so she could contact the phone carrier.

A few moments later, she hung up. "I have to go to the store near Penn Station. It's the one that handles repairs. It might not be quick if I'm repairing the screen or getting a replacement phone."

Anne reassured her, "Don't worry. It might just be an issue with the battery or a simple phone replacement. You are our guest and very welcome here. I hope it gets sorted easily for you." Anne's expression seemed to hint at a deeper understanding or perhaps a silent appreciation for the moment they were sharing.

Anna turned to Emma. "My husband will be home soon. He's a superintendent of a high rise in the city. Go sit, make yourself at home."

Emma moved to the living room, where she saw some framed photos on the walls. There was a framed photo of a man proudly holding an Employee of the Year award to Theodore Garcia. Another photo captured him surrounded by kids at the Y, his warm smile reflecting his dedication to mentoring the youth in the community. Lots of family pictures decorated the wall.

Ryan's uncle walked through the door just as Emma heard the oven timer go off in the kitchen. He looked up and saw her in his living room.

When Emma's eyes met him, she smiled. "Hi, Mr. Garcia," she said, stepping forward, holding out her hand. "I'm Emma Duque. Ryan brought me here." She could tell him she was a friend of Ryan's. They had just met.

"Please. Call me Theo." He shook her hand back and studied her face before he said, "Have we met before? I get this odd feeling I know you."

"No. I don't think so." And Emma wondered if more magical things were going on, and he was feeling it. "I have one of those familiar faces." She turned toward the photos on the wall. "I was just looking at your photo gallery. You have an incredible family." There was the couple's wedding portrait. The photo exuded a palpable aura of love.

Just then, Anne walked into the room and overheard their conversation. Her face lit up with pride as she heard Emma's compliment.

Emma noticed three children in the family photos and remarked, "You have three beautiful children."

Anne smiled warmly and replied, "Yes, our youngest, Matthew, who is just five years old, is asleep right now. He is feeling under the weather."

Ryan came back into the living room. He had changed into a pair of sweatpants and a T-shirt. He looked great. Then she noticed a warmth spread across his cheeks as he caught sight of her, which made her smile. She wondered if he was thinking the same thing as she was.

Appearing to compose himself quickly, Ryan greeted his uncle Theo, saying, "Hey, Uncle Theo! How's it going?"

"Great. How's the hospital? Still keeping you busy. You haven't been home early enough for dinner for a while."

"Yes. It's good. Busy. My vacation starts today."

Anne looked at Theo and smiled, then at Ryan and Emma. "Dinner is ready."

Before they turned toward the kitchen, Anne and Theo caught each other's eyes and smiled knowingly, aware that something romantic was happening.

Chapter 11

Dinner

"Let's take our seats," Theo said, settling at the head of the table with Anne on his right. He motioned for Emma to sit on his other side while Ryan sat beside her. Alyssa and Alex took their seats.

"Thank you, Lord, for gathering us and blessing the food we are about to eat. Please provide for those in need," Theo said.

"Amen!" they all replied in perfect harmony.

"It's time to eat," he announced, passing the serving plate of chicken to Emma. "Visitors first," he added with a wink.

As they ate, it became clear how special this family was, as the love emanating from each family member became palpable. Even at that moment, she could feel the empath within her rejoicing. Despite not remembering where she had been going when she was pushed and hit her head, she felt safe and confident that she was in the right place.

Anne turned to her, her eyes curious. "So, Emma, what do you do for a living?"

"I have a website called Anita Inspires. I post quotes and words of inspiration to help people."

Theo's eyes narrowed slightly, a hint of amusement flickering in them, akin to the way the Rock arches one eyebrow. "Do you sell anything on it?"

"Yes, I do. It is named after my ancestor, Anita Paz. I sell cleansing kits, crystals, and other items for your body, mind, and spirit."

"Oh, that sounds fascinating," Anne remarked with a quizzical expression. Ryan met Emma's gaze, mirroring Anne's interest.

As Theo absorbed this revelation, his brow furrowed slightly. "How do these products help people?"

"The things I sell can help you remove negative influences from your home. Similar to the incense used in churches, they can create a sacred space for meditation and spiritual living. The body, mind, and spirit market are steadily growing as people seek different ways to heal. I've been in this business since I graduated from college, and while it's had its challenges, I've learned a lot about online sales and the needs of my customers."

Ryan, always the pragmatist, asked, "Do people really buy into this kind of thing?" His tone was sincere and respectful.

Emma's eyes softened. "Yes, they do. Consider the rituals at churches, where the priest cleanses the entrance with incense as people enter and leave. I sell the same kinds of cleansing products on my website, the same items used in your church."

Anne nodded thoughtfully. "It's unconventional, but intriguing, nonetheless. I suppose there's a market for everything."

"So, by using what you sell," Theo mused, "one can shut out all the bad stuff."

Emma wore a beaming smile as she spoke to him, "Exactly. It's like creating a haven within your home that brings in positive energy and light to uplift you. It allows one to manifest things. You can radiate positivity to others through your own light and create a serene and relaxing environment. By embracing herbs like Rue or *Ruda*, you can cleanse your space and bring in good luck to manifest and create an even more positive atmosphere within your home."

Theo leaned in toward Anne, whispering with a napkin over his mouth but Emma heard him. "I thought she was just another fruitcake, and I wanted to see what kind of nonsense she'd come up with but..."

"She is different," Anne whispered back.

So, Emma set out to win them over, to gently educate them as she often did with skeptics. Before long her profound insight left the others slightly stunned. They talked more, asked questions, clearly taking her seriously as her ability to tap into the spiritual essence, to captivate them, continued throughout the night. She had a way with words, her knowledge evident as she engaged in spirited debates, articulating both sides.

After they all finished their meals, including the wonderful chocolate cake Anna had made for dessert, Alex cleared the table and Anne checked on the soup she had made for Matthew, who had fallen sick with sniffles. Theo excused himself as he went to check on Matthew, and ten-year-old Alyssa chattered on and on about things that happened in summer school that day.

Alex grumbled at Alyssa, "Can you please stop talking? My ears are hurting." He covered his ears with his hands and stuck his tongue out at her, teasing his little sister.

Alyssa rolled her eyes, stuck her tongue back at him, and said, "Grow up, Alex," prompting Anne to intervene.

She looked at them and said sternly, "Oh, stop it! Both of you. Be nice to each other. Also, get ready for bed soon. You have school tomorrow."

Alex and Alyssa turned to Ryan and Emma and told them both "goodnight" and left.

"Thank you for dinner, "Emma told Anne. "The food was delicious. You've all been so welcoming,"

"*De nada,* we are glad to have you," Anne replied, picking up a tray of food. Make yourself at home while I take this to Matthew." With a glance to make certain everything was in order, she left the room, her steps steady and deliberate.

And Emma looked at Ryan and smiled.

With a glance to make sure everything was in order, Anne picked up the tray and headed toward Matthew's room, her steps steady and deliberate.

Ryan had watched as Emma easily interacted with his family. He could not take his eyes off her and felt something stirring inside him, especially when she smiled at him as she was.

What is it about Emma?

All he knew was that he wanted to learn more about her. "So, I guess you have another full-time job besides the website," Ryan said quickly, trying to make conversation.

"No, that is my only job. I actually make decent money from it and social media because of affiliate links and ads. Over the years, people have become more and more interested in the mind, body, and spirit. This spirituality is not only good for business, but it also makes me happy to help others," Emma said.

"Of course, sorry," Ryan said. "I didn't mean for it to sound like an idiot. I imagine it does make money. A friend of mine has a medical podcast, and he also makes money using affiliate links. I bet that you flourish at whatever you put your mind to."

When he finished speaking, he noticed Emma looking back at him, and they locked eyes for a moment. In that very moment, Ryan felt lost in her gaze. Butterflies flapped in his stomach, and his heart felt like it was pounding one hundred times a second.

Emma tried not to stare at Ryan, but her eyes met his hazel eyes briefly before she looked away. She could sense the intensity of his gaze, and electricity seemed to spark between them. A subtle shift occurred at that moment, and an unspoken recognition of mutual attraction began to bloom. Emma felt his gaze linger. The moment was surprising to her, yet undeniably intriguing.

Alyssa walked in just then to get a glass of water and asked Emma in bewilderment, "Are you okay?"

"What?" Emma asked.

"You look like a statue," Alyssa said.

Emma started coughing, embarrassed, and grabbed the glass of water on the table.

Alyssa got her glass of water and left the kitchen.

"Are you okay?" Ryan leaned forward, his expression serious.

Emma gulped more water. "I'm fine." But she could feel her face flush.

"I want to check that bump on your head to be safe." Ryan stepped closer.

Emma nodded, wincing slightly as Ryan gently examined the swollen bump.

"Sorry," Ryan said softly, his touch gentle. "Remember I'm a doctor, so I just want to make sure everything's okay."

He told her to breathe slowly, and she complied, her eyes fixed on him as his calm, reassuring words comforted her, making her think he must be good at his job.

"Give me your hand," Ryan said calmly. Emma complied, and Ryan lightly guided her hand to feel the bump. "This is swollen. Do you feel how it's raised?"

Emma responded with a soft expression. "Yes."

"When you wake up tomorrow, check it again. Let me know if it hasn't gone down, and we'll take another look. If you're concerned, it's best to see your doctor immediately," Ryan advised.

"Do you think it won't go down?" Emma asked, her voice tinged with worry.

"No, it should go down. Just put an ice pack on it before you go to sleep," Ryan reassured her.

All this time, Ryan still held her hand.

Emma smiled and asked, "Can I have my hand back now? I'm okay."

Ryan promptly released her hand.

They stood there in silence as something passed between them. Emma sensed a connection she had never felt, one that was surprisingly deep for two people who had just met.

CHAPTER 12

THE GIFT

Despite the late hour, neither Ryan nor Emma showed any signs of wanting to call it a night. They settled onto the couch as they talked about family.

Ryan told her about his mother, Luna, and Emma noticed a framed photo nearby. It was a picture of Ryan standing between a beautiful older woman she recognized and a younger woman.

"That's my mom," Ryan said, pointing to the photo. "At my medical school graduation. She passed away from cancer a few years ago."

Emma turned to him. "When you left me at the door to get money for the taxi, the door opened, and an older lady spoke to me and said, 'We were waiting for you,' and she also wanted me to tell you that she was proud of her *chichi*."

His eyes widened in disbelief as he picked up his mother's picture. He turned to Emma with a shocked expression on his face. "Was this the woman you saw?"

"Yes." Emma cleared her throat and decided she needed to share a bit more about herself.

She took a deep breath, feeling Ryan's mother's presence. She could see her spirit materialize, her ethereal form shimmering slightly as she stood with a serene expression.

"I am intuitive. Or, as some would say, a psychic medium. I can talk to the spirits of loved ones who have passed," Emma began, her voice soft but steady. "Do not be scared, but your mom is here right now. I believe she has something important to say."

Ryan looked shocked, but he nodded and asked hesitantly, "Okay...What is it?"

Emma paused momentarily, listening to the spirit, before turning to Ryan with a gentle smile. "She said you asked her a question. And the answer is yes, but when you least expect it."

Ryan's face turned pale, his eyes glistening with unshed tears.

"What was the question you asked her?" Emma asked, her voice tender and understanding.

Tears began to flow freely down Ryan's cheeks as he heard the message. He quickly wiped them away and said, "The question wasn't important." His voice was shaky, and Emma could see the raw emotion in his eyes. Sensing his need for space, Emma didn't push further.

Ryan stood abruptly from the sofa, his movements stiff and uneasy. "I will be right back. Excuse me," he said quickly, almost stumbling over his words.

Emma watched him as he exited the room. It was a common response whenever she revealed her gift. She trusted him enough to reveal her truth. She hoped Ryan wouldn't be like some others who had tried to use her abilities for their own gain.

In her brief time with Ryan and his family, she had sensed

his mother's protective presence around him. She could feel the warmth and love that emanated from the spirit, and from that love, she believed that Ryan was different. But the fear of being manipulated for her gift lingered, a shadow she couldn't shake. She knew that her abilities were a blessing, but they also made her vulnerable in ways most people couldn't understand.

Emma glanced around the room, taking in the cozy setting. The soft glow of the table lamp cast a warm light, and the scent of the cake Anne baked lingered in the air. She could hear the faint hum of the refrigerator and the distant sound of a TV from another room. The normalcy of the environment contrasted sharply with the extraordinary nature of her abilities, grounding her in the present moment.

CHAPTER 13

A Hint of Romance & Sexy Fall

Ryan entered the bathroom feeling numb and unable to process what had just happened. He turned on the cold tap and bent over the sink, cupping his hands to splash water over his face. He knew he had been alone in his room when he asked his mother that question, so there was no way Emma could know what he wanted.

A million questions and emotions streamed through his mind like a raging river. He dried his face with a towel, feeling the cold fabric against his skin. A chill ran down his spine as he began to accept that it must really have been some spiritual sign from his mother. He knew it, and now he felt it. But he was a doctor, wasn't he, a man of science?

Ryan returned to Emma and casually asked, "What are you doing tomorrow?"

Emma rubbed her forehead, trying to piece together her plans. "Well, I might see a doctor if the swelling on my head hasn't gone down. And I need to get my phone fixed. Once that's done, I might have to head out if I get a call. Beyond that, I'm not sure yet."

Ryan considered the suggestion. "We should take the train together since we're going in the same direction. I'm meeting my sister later in the city, and I could use some help picking a wedding gift for her since I'm not good at it. And Macy's is near Penn Station."

Emma smiled, feeling a sense of relief at the prospect of company. "Yes. I'd be happy to help."

As Ryan walked toward the kitchen, he turned back to her, "I'm getting you an ice bag for your head."

Emma winced slightly, pressing her hand to her forehead. "Thank you," she said quietly, her eyes reflecting her discomfort and relief at the thought of the cold compress.

He returned with the ice pack and a cold bottle of water. "Here. This should help with the swelling," he said, handing her the ice pack and the water. "You need to take the pain med they gave you.

"Thank you," she said softly, accepting both. Her face softened in appreciation. She took her medication, then applied the ice pack gently to her head, feeling the cool relief. "The ice feels good," she said softly. "So your sister is getting married?"

Ryan's face relaxed. "They eloped recently. So to appease Jacob's family, who were unhappy that they chose to elope, they are having a church ceremony with a small reception in the church basement. Jacob's parents are older and quite traditional."

"My sister is getting married, too," Emma said, a small smile tugging at her lips. "What a coincidence."

"Small world, right?" Ryan said. "Mia wanted to celebrate longer, a real reception for friends and family, and since Jacob's parents don't stay out late, Theo suggested hosting an after-party at our place. So, there will be a lot of celebrations."

Ryan glanced at the clock. "I'm meeting Mia tomorrow at 10:00 a.m."

Emma yawned. "Sorry. It's already after midnight. I should head to bed," she said, standing.

Ryan stood up as well, being the gentleman he had been since she ran into him. "Goodnight," he said.

Emma gave him a small, understanding smile, her eyes softening. She headed toward the bedroom, her steps slow and deliberate, the weight of the day's events finally catching up with her.

As she disappeared down the hallway, Ryan paused momentarily, his thoughts lingering on their conversation before he, too, prepared for sleep. He opted to sleep on the sofa bed in the living room rather than bothering with the airbed. Before he got into bed, he glanced toward his bedroom door, hoping he hadn't left anything embarrassing in there despite tidying up earlier. He found having a pretty woman he barely knew using his room amusing and awkward.

As he settled onto the sofa bed, he couldn't help but chuckle at the absurdity of it all. Ryan let out a contented sigh, his eyes lingering on the fading glow of the lamp. Memories of his conversation with Emma danced through his mind. As he closed his eyes, her laughter echoed in his thoughts, and he welcomed the warmth of her presence in his dreams throughout the night.

Ryan blinked against the brightness of the morning sun. Heavy with a languid sense of relaxation, his limbs shifted on something soft beneath him. A beach towel, he realized, as his senses sharpened to the sound of surf whispering secrets to the shore.

He propped himself up on one elbow, while his gaze swept across an expanse of the beach so pristine it could only exist in dreams or postcards. The sky was a canvas of unmarred blue, save for the sun, a radiant orb pouring its golden essence onto the sands below, painting everything in hues of amber and honey.

Dressed only in blue swim trunks that clung to his frame, Ryan felt how the golden glow of the sun warmed his skin. The ocean's breath caressed his face, carrying the scent of salt, lulling him deeper into this surreal serenity.

As he rolled onto his side, the sight that greeted him stole the breath from his lungs. Emma. There she was, mere inches from him, her presence a beacon of beauty and desire. She lay with effortless grace, her skin a testament to the sun's affection, bronzed and glistening as if she were sculpted from the beach itself. The white bikini she wore left little to the imagination.

His heart skipped a beat for a moment, caught in the gravity of her allure. Then, as if sensing his stare, Emma turned toward him. Her lips curved into a smile that could've rivaled the brilliance of the day, and her light brown eyes, clear and full of warmth, sparkled with a light that seemed to mirror the waves behind her. The lapping of the waves seemed to harmonize with Emma's voice as she spoke, pulling Ryan further from the arms of slumber.

"Hi, sleepyhead," she said, her tone a gentle melody that blended seamlessly with the tranquil surroundings. "I was wondering when you would wake up."

Ryan rubbed at his eyes as his vision cleared and focused on

Emma's radiant face, he couldn't help but smile back, captivated by the playful glint in her eyes.

"Oh, you were? Why?" he asked, his voice rough with the remnants of dreams yet to be forgotten. The curiosity that tinged his question was genuine, driven by a desire to understand her presence in this place that felt both foreign and familiar.

The sun's warmth wrapped around him like a comforting blanket, but Emma's proximity set his senses ablaze. She leaned in, the scent of coconut and sea salt mingling as she brought her pink lips tantalizingly close to his ear. Her whisper brushed against him, intimate and with an invitation that sent a shiver down his spine. "I need help putting sunblock all over my body."

Each word was a siren's call, stirring something primal within him. He felt the heat from her breath, the faintest touch igniting a wildfire of anticipation. His heart hammered against his ribcage, a drumbeat urging him closer.

"Then I'm the man for you," he responded, the words emerging in a deep, sultry tone that mirrored the hunger in his gaze.

Desire pulsed through his veins, thrumming with the same rhythm as the ocean's waves. He was lost in the moment, in the depth of her eyes, and the promise of her smile.

With the smooth white bottle now in his possession, he pressed its sides, coaxing a generous dollop of sunblock into his palm. The creamy substance was cool, almost cold, against his skin, contrasting with the heat of the midday sun overhead. He smeared the lotion between his hands, prepping it for application.

"Ready?" His voice carried a hint of playfulness mingling with the undercurrent of desire that hadn't ebbed since her initial request.

"Always," she replied, her tone matching his.

He began at her shoulders, where speckles of sunlight danced through the canopy of a nearby palm. His fingers moved with practiced care, tracing the lines of her muscles beneath the surface of her bronzed skin. As he massaged the lotion in, each stroke sent ripples of contentment through Emma's frame, and the tension seemed to melt away from her body, absorbed by the sand below.

Her shoulders were smooth, and the curves and contours were familiar to his touch, yet he found himself exploring them as if it were the first time. His own heartbeat became a beat pulsing in his ears, keeping time with the methodical movement of his hands, each beat a reminder of the thin line they tread between intimacy and restraint.

The silence around them was broken only by the soft hush of waves, a soothing backdrop to the charged atmosphere that cocooned the pair. Emma's soft smile served as his anchor as he ventured further. His palms slipped down to the small of her back, fingertips grazing the edges of her bikini tie.

There, his touch grew bolder, more assertive, as he spread the sunblock over the gentle swell of her lower back. The sensation of her skin, hot from the sun but cool where the lotion kissed it, was intoxicating. Her breath hitched slightly, barely audible above the whisper of the sea.

He continued, gliding effortlessly over the curves of her hips and down the length of her thighs. Her muscles tensed briefly under the pressure of his hands, then relaxed as he worked the lotion into her skin. Each movement brought him closer to the warmth radiating from her, a sexy reminder of the intimate caress of his hands.

His fingers ventured higher, tracing the inside of her thighs with a featherlight touch, daring in its proximity to unspoken promises. Emma's body responded, a quiet shiver passing through her as he navigated the sensitive territory, her trust in him as palpable as the warmth of her flesh.

Finally, his hands circled back to her abdomen, moving in gentle patterns as he applied the sunblock. His fingers hovered just above the rise of her breasts, careful yet confident in their ministrations. The delicate brush of his knuckles against the underside of her breasts was enough to elicit another soft exhale from Emma's parted lips.

The air between them seemed to pulse with energy, each breath, each caress weaving an invisible thread that pulled them inexorably closer. In this moment, they were all that existed, two figures etched against the canvas of a dream.

As his hands lingered near the swell of her hips, her breathing grew heavier, rising and falling in a rhythm that matched the distant waves. She released a deep sigh of pleasure, her body tingling with intensity. Her dark brown hair and blonde ombre tips sprawled across the towel, framing her face in a halo of golden-tinged strands. She opened her eyes slowly, revealing the lust she was feeling. In those depths, he saw an echo of his own longing reflected back at him, magnified and raw. "Ryan…" The tone of her voice spoke of a need, a deep longing for him. She pulled him toward her, closing the distance between their bodies. The sultry allure of her skin beckoned him, an irresistible siren's call that promised oblivion in its touch.

"Kiss me," she breathed, her words tinged with urgency as

she guided his hand back to the apex of her thighs. "Right there where your hands are." The request hung in the air, heavy with anticipation. He hesitated for a fraction of a heartbeat, caught in the gravity of the moment. But the pull of desire was too strong, the yearning in her gaze impossible to resist. He moved closer, his fingers retracing the path they had just traveled, now armed with a new, intimate purpose.

Leaning forward, he pressed his lips against the soft fabric of her bikini, just where the heat of her body called him most fiercely. The kiss was a silent pledge, a testament to their unspoken connection. Her sharp intake of breath served as both encouragement and plea, spurring him on in the dreamlike place together on this isolated stretch of paradise.

His gaze locked onto hers, his breath catching as the reality of her invitation sunk in. A surge of heat coursed through him, igniting every nerve with electric anticipation. With trembling hands, he caressed the smooth curve of her hip, marveling at the softness of her sun-kissed skin beneath his touch. Leaning closer, his lips met the delicate fabric of her bikini with a tenderness that sent his pulse racing.

The gentle pressure of his mouth against her stirred a response in her body, a subtle arching toward him that spoke volumes. Encouraged by her reaction, his kisses grew bolder, tracing a path along the contours of her abdomen. Each kiss was a confession of the desire he had started to manifest. As a moan escaped her lips, she beckoned him to continue.

Hearing her moan stirred a deep need within him. Their attraction was palpable, each drawn to the other with equal intensity.

As he ascended her torso, his lips brushed against the underside of her breasts, sending shivers of longing through both of them. The moment's intimacy swelled within him, blooming like a night flower as he prepared to claim her lips in a kiss that promised to sear their very souls.

But before their mouths could meet, the world abruptly spun away. There was a jolt, a disorienting sensation of falling...

He hit the living room floor with an ungainly thud, the impact jarring him from head to toe. The dream beach had evaporated, whisked away by the chill of the waking world.

"Fucking *mierda*." He groaned, wincing as he registered the discomfort of his awkward landing. Disoriented, he took a moment to acknowledge the painful proof of his arousal, pressing urgently against the confines of his shorts. With a heavy sigh, he pushed himself into a sitting position, the remnants of the dream fading like mist in the morning sun. His hand raked through his tousled hair as he tried to calm the wild thrumming of his heart.

The vivid and intoxicating memory of Emma clung to him, a haunting echo of what might have been.

"*Coño*." With a grunt, he hoisted himself off the cold floor and sat on the sofa bed. His hands smoothed out the creases in the sheets, then plumped the pillows in a vain attempt to craft some semblance of comfort. As he lay back, the fabric sighed beneath him, and he relaxed. The ghost of Emma's smile lingered in his mind's eye, the curve of her lips more tangible than the pillow under his head. He let out a sigh, the sound lost in the stillness of the room. Her image danced behind his closed lids, the dream of her so vivid it was as though he could reach out and touch her once again.

With a deliberate effort, he shut out the world around him,

seeking solace in the steady rhythm of his breath. Slowly, the room, the discomfort, and the lingering embarrassment faded into the background as sleep reclaimed him. He drifted, on the verge of dreams, where the promise of Emma's touch awaited, a beacon in the night guiding him back to that perfect beach.

CHAPTER 14

SWEET DREAMS & TEMPTING FANTASIES

Emma could not sleep as she lay in Ryan's bed. She thought of all that had happened since she got off the train. Oh, how she wished she had sage to give herself a cleansing bath, which always calmed her down. Her mind raced with remembered thoughts...her broken phone, the upcoming maid of honor dress shopping with Liz. Her body refused to relax, tension knotting her muscles and keeping her awake. Remembering her grandmother Ariana's advice, Emma took three deep breaths, feeling the day's stress begin to melt away and she finally drifted off to sleep.

As slumber's veil descended, the world around Emma rippled and transformed. In her dream, she found herself in a cozy Airbnb, the walls of the bedroom dissolving into a picturesque outdoor retreat, where the warm caress of the sun draped over her on a comfortable outdoor lounger.

Surrounding her was a serene Zen Garden with a sparkling pool reflecting the clear blue sky. On one side of the garden, vibrant sunflowers swayed gently in the breeze, their golden faces beaming in the sunlight. On the other side, lush rose bushes bloomed in rich colors, their delicate petals fluttering slightly in the breeze.

A tall tree stood majestically at the garden's edge, its leaves rustling softly with each small gust of wind. Birds flew overhead, their cheerful chirps adding a musical background to the tranquil scene. As she lay on the lounger, feeling the sun's warmth envelop her in a soothing embrace, she basked in the beauty of this dreamlike oasis.

Her eyes fluttered open, adjusting to the brightness of the dream world. She looked down and found herself wearing a white bikini, the tanning cream on her skin glistening under the golden rays. The yard stretched out before her, yet something was amiss.

Her gaze fell upon the man lying face down on the lounger beside her as she surveyed her surroundings. Blue shorts adorned hugged his hips while his bare back showcased a striking tattoo of a lion's face. Curiosity piqued, her eyes wandered over his sculpted back and toned butt, appreciating the view with a mix of admiration and intrigue.

Unable to resist, she gently poked the man's shoulder. As she settled back into her lounger, he stirred and turned to face her, then sat up. Shock and delight intermingled as recognition dawned. It was Ryan. His captivating hazel eyes were even more mesmerizing in the sunlight's glow.

She drank in the sight of him, her eyes roving over his muscular chest. The urge to touch him, to explore every inch of his sun-kissed skin, surged through her veins. Ryan's lips curved into a knowing smile, his eyes glinting with mischief.

"Do you like what you see, Emma?" he asked, his voice a husky whisper that sent shivers down her spine.

She nodded, her tongue darting out to moisten her

suddenly dry lips. "Definitely," she breathed out, her heart pounding an erratic rhythm in her chest.

Ryan's smile widened, his body language exuding an irresistible magnetism that pulled her in, like the moon drawing the tide.

"Then why don't you come over here and touch me?" he invited, patting his lap in a gesture that was both playful and seductive. Her hesitation vanished, swept away by the tide of desire that crashed over her. She rose from her chair stood between Ryan's muscular legs, her hands resting on his shoulders and heart fluttering with anticipation. As if in a dream, she moved one hand onto his chiseled chest, marveling at the firmness beneath her fingertips. Her other hand came to rest over his heart, feeling its steady rhythm as she gazed into his eyes, searching for his reaction.

Ryan's eyelids fluttered closed, a contented sigh escaping his lips. "Just a little farther down," he murmured, his voice thick with desire.

Her hands began a tantalizing journey down his torso, her touch feather light as she traced the contours of his abs.

"A little more," Ryan encouraged, his breath hitching in his throat.

Finally, her hands reached their destination, coming to rest atop his arousal straining against his swimming trunks. *Oh my god, this is really happening.* Her heart pounded in her ears. His arousal was unmistakable, and she marveled at his size.

Stimulated by the heat of the moment, she turned the tables on Ryan. "Your turn," she purred, guiding his hands to her chest. "Like this."

Ryan's strong hands cupped her breasts, his touch sending electric sparks through her body.

"Yes, just like that," she gasped, arching into his touch. "Now, be a good boy and go all the way down," she instructed, her voice husky with need.

"Your wish is my command," he growled, his touch igniting a fire deep within her. His eyes darkened with desire as his hands traveled south, his fingers dancing over her smooth skin.

As his skilled fingers found her most sensitive spot, she couldn't contain her moans of pleasure. "Your hands are magical," she whispered, her hips rocking against his touch.

Ryan's gaze locked with hers, the intensity of his wanton desire nearly stealing her breath. He increased the speed and pressure of his fingers, driving her closer and closer to the edge. Her cries of ecstasy filled the air as she tumbled over the breaking point, her body shuddering with the force of her climax.

"Yes! Yes! Yes!" she screamed, collapsing against Ryan's chest as the waves of pleasure crashed over her.

"Now it's my turn," he declared, his voice full of promise.

Emma awoke suddenly, her dream gone, but her body still trembling from the aftershocks of her intense orgasm. She blinked, disoriented, as she realized she was in bed, alone.

A satisfied smile played on her lips.

That was the wettest dream she'd had in a long time, she mused, rolling over and snuggling into her pillow. She drifted back to sleep with a contented sigh, her mind still buzzing with the delicious memories of her fantasy encounter with Ryan.

CHAPTER 15

DREAMS & DIVINE INTERVENTIONS

The next morning, Emma woke up feeling rejuvenated but also a little frustrated. The lucid dream about Ryan had left her with a lingering need and a racing heart. She knew she needed to find a way to quench the fire that Ryan had reignited in her, dream or not. As she lay in bed, she pondered the nature of her feelings. Was she truly developing feelings for him, or was it lust clouding her judgment?

Her mind replayed the dream, the way Ryan's hazel eyes shone in the sunlight, his body, and the tender way he had touched her. She sighed, realizing that her thoughts were not just about his physical appeal but also about the comfort and connection she felt in his presence. She couldn't help but wonder if there was something deeper between them, something worth exploring.

She took a shower, letting the warm water wash away any lingering sleepiness. She felt the bump on her head, which was tender, but the swelling was going down. That was good.

After getting dressed, she made her way down the hall to a door that led outside to the backyard. The fresh dew on the grass felt cool under her feet. She found a comfortable spot on the grass and sat. Opening her bag, she took out her selenite crystal to cleanse herself, feeling its soothing energy envelop her as she prepared for the new day ahead.

She closed her eyes, letting the sounds of nature and the sun's warmth guide her into a peaceful meditation.

Soon a vision formed. She saw herself giving a can of formula and water to a woman on the subway platform. The woman was pleading for food to feed her baby, but no one was stepping up to help her. "Please help me," the woman repeated several times. But everyone around her was in a hurry and dismissed her.

The vision faded with Emma feeling overwhelmed with compassion. She took this information to heart and understood she would need to help this woman whenever that would be.

After sitting for a few more minutes, Emma got up to return inside. When she made her way to the kitchen, she saw Ryan awake and ready to go. Her cheeks turned red as she thought of her dream. She looked up again and noticed that Ryan's cheeks were also red.

"Morning!" she said.

"*Buenos días!* I hope you had a restful sleep last night," Ryan said.

"Yes, I did. Funny thing is, I dreamt of you last night."

"You did?" Ryan said, "That's a coincidence. I had a dream about you, too. What was your dream about?"

"Tell me about your dream," Emma asked.

"Well, I did ask you first."

"I dreamed we were in an Airbnb, sitting in the backyard getting a tan."

"Oh, I dreamed we were both at the beach and getting a tan, too." He chuckled.

As Emma glanced up and saw the mischievous twinkle in his eyes, his cheeks turned red again.

"I'm guessing we both need a little R & R in a sunny place."

"Well," she said, changing the conversation. "We should go."

Ryan and Emma walked out of the house and headed for the subway. The sky was clear, the air already heating up with the sticky summer warmth. Up and down the block, houses were decorated for the Fourth of July. Flags waved in the breeze, and every porch looked like it had been styled from a Pinterest board titled "Fourth of July."

"These houses are beautiful," Emma said, slowing to take it all in. "It's like everyone got the same memo...and dressed up their homes with Fourth of July gear."

Ryan smiled. "Every year, the Lopezes, two blocks down, set up this giant inflatable projector screen and show a movie in their driveway. It's a neighborhood tradition now."

Emma blinked. "In the driveway?"

"Yep. Everyone brings lawn chairs and snacks. Last year they played Elf."

Emma lit up. "Stop. That is my favorite movie of all time. I quote Buddy the Elf way more than I should admit."

Ryan raised an eyebrow. "Really? Got a favorite line?"

"Easy. Cotton headed ninny muggins."

He laughed.

They continued walking toward the subway, passing a row of houses draped with American flag bunting over the fences and gates.

"My mom, sister, and I used to go see the Macy's fireworks

every year," Ryan said. "We would get there early with our little fold-up chairs, sandwiches wrapped in foil, and those fans from the dollar store that just made noise."

Emma gave him a playful nudge. "Classic."

"One year, it rained. Most people packed up, but we stayed. We had on our rain jackets and held umbrellas while my mom just sat there and said, 'Freedom came at a price. A little rain is nothing.' When the fireworks finally started, the lights reflected off the wet pavement. It looked like magic."

Emma's voice softened. "That's beautiful."

"My sister Liz brought me to see them once at Astoria Park," Emma said.

"We had snacks, pop-up chairs, and a front-row view. It was loud, colorful, and totally unforgettable night."

Their eyes met. There was something in the air between them, light but undeniable.

Ryan looked ahead and said quietly, "You don't realize they're the good old days until they're gone. I didn't realize how much I'd miss it...Now that my mom's not here anymore."

Emma tucked a loose strand of hair behind her ear. "Maybe we should start collecting new ones."

Ryan looked at her and smiled. "Yeah. I'm good with that."

They kept walking toward the subway, a few early fireworks crackling somewhere in the distance.

As they neared a bodega by the subway stairs, Ryan stopped and turned to Emma. "Hey, do you need anything? I'm going to grab a bottle of water."

Emma pulled forty dollars from her bag and handed it to him. "Yeah, can you get me a can of baby formula and a bottle of water?"

Ryan raised an eyebrow, clearly confused but not pushing.

"It's important," she said. "I had a vision I would need it."

He nodded without hesitation. "No worries. I can do that. Want anything else?"

Emma thought for a moment, then shook her head. "No, thanks. I'll wait out here."

While Ryan was inside, Emma leaned against the bodega wall with her arms crossed. The shop was packed and loud. Outside, the morning air felt refreshing and was a reprieve from the crowded bodega.

"Emma!"

Her name rang out from across the street. She looked up, her eyes catching a familiar face emerging through the light. Gary Walters, her sister's fiancé, was walking toward her,

"Hey!" Gary said as if he had come closer. "Fancy running into you here. How've you been?"

"I'm alright," Emma replied, keeping her tone light. "Had some bad luck with my phone. It's not working. There was an incident on the train platform yesterday. She wasn't about to tell him about the injury. Her sister would be in full panic mode if she found out. So, she brushed it off, trying to seem casual. "Anyway, I'm heading to get it fixed in the city." She pulled the phone out of her bag and showed it to him quickly. "I can't access my contacts."

Gary glanced at the phone and then back at her. "Do you need Liz's info? I can give it to you."

"Actually, yeah, that'd be great," Emma said. Gary dug into his pocket, pulled out a scrap of paper, and quickly wrote down Liz's cell number, address and badge number. Emma took it with a sigh of relief and slid it into her pocket.

"And one more thing," she added. "I have a question. I had to show my ID yesterday as a witness and I forgot to get it back.

I think officer at Penn Station had my ID. Can I just go and ask for it back?"

"No problem," Gary said, giving her a reassuring smile. "Just to be sure, I'll call them when I get back to the precinct so they know you are Liz's sister."

"Thanks, Gary. I really appreciate it," Emma said, feeling more at ease now that Gary was on it. Knowing she'd have her home address, plus Liz's number, helped ease her nerves. For the first time that morning, Emma felt like things were starting to get back under control.

Ryan stepped out of the bodega to see Emma talking with a tall guy and laughing. A flicker of unease tugged at him. He watched as she smiled at the man and put her hand on his arm. Her laughter was light, ringing in the air.

Who is this guy? Ryan thought to himself. He was surprised by his sudden feeling of jealousy as he stepped closer to them after seeing her put her hands on him. Did Emma mean enough to him already that he could be jealous?

"Ryan," Emma said when she saw him. "Hey, I want you to meet Gary Walters. Gary, this is Ryan Garcia."

Gary looked at Ryan, assessing, and firmly shook his hand. "Nice to meet you," he said politely.

Ryan leveled his gaze at Gary and nodded curtly. "Likewise," he replied coolly before returning his attention to Emma, where they both checked each other out with a subtle, lingering gaze.

Gary cleared his throat and gestured to the parked patrol car on the street. "Well, I have to get back to work, but I'll see you later," he promised with a wink.

Emma beamed at him and waved goodbye as he walked away. Ryan kept his face emotionless, not wanting her to know how much Gary's presence had bothered him. *But why does it bother me so much?*

Emma turned back to Ryan after Gary drove away.

Ryan was staring at the street.

"We can go," Emma told him. She waved her hands in front of Ryan's face, calling, "Earth to Ryan! Come on! Let's go!"

Jolted, Ryan responded, "Oh! Sorry about that. Let's go catch the train."

Emma smiled, but something mischievous was in her eyes. "Yes, let's go," she said as they descended the nearby subway steps. They swiped their cards and hopped onto the train that had just arrived.

Ryan was curious as he followed her. How did she know Gary? What were they talking about? He tried to hide his jealousy, not wanting her to discover how envious he was.

Ryan took a seat on the train, and Emma did, too. He could not take his eyes off her.

"So, who is Gary?" he asked with a hint of challenge in his voice.

Emma shrugged. "He's a police officer in the Precinct," she answered.

"So, what is going on with you two?"

Emma Moment: *Me thinks someone is jealous. It's cute.*

"Gary is my sister's fiancé. I asked him if he could give me her number since my cell is out of commission and help get my ID back," she told him.

"So, you aren't seeing anyone?" Ryan asked, his body tense, mostly because this was the first time he had ever felt jealous of another guy.

After a moment, she responded with a teasing glint in her eye. "No. And what about you? Are you seeing anyone?"

Ryan sighed, shaking his head. "No."

Emma took a moment to make eye contact with him, her expression softening. She smiled softly. "I'm glad," she admitted.

Ryan didn't know what to say. He was still feeling emotions he hadn't felt before.

Emma turned to Ryan and said, "My sister, Liz, is a police officer. She met Gary on the job. If I'm not very forthcoming, it's because I am cautious. I'm intuitive. It's hard for me to know if people like me for me or for my gift. I've had trouble in the past."

He asked, "Does your sister, your family, all have the gift?"

"Yeah," Emma said. "We are all intuitive. It has been passed down from my mom's side of the family from generation to generation."

Ryan's expression grew thoughtful as he considered Emma's words. He had never met anyone like Emma. She was beautiful with a kind heart and a deep, spiritual insight into the world.

Realizing she had been talking for a while, Emma paused, noticing that Ryan's eyes were closed. She felt a pang of self-awareness and tried to read his expression, but his features remained unreadable, hidden behind his calm demeanor.

"Ryan?" Emma repeated, this time playfully hitting his arm with her elbow to wake him up.

He looked at her. "Sorry," he said. "I was just taking in what you were just saying."

She looked at him. "Have you ever experienced something paranormal?"

"I don't think so."

Emma nodded, understanding. "I do it all the time. Sometimes, it is hard to believe in things we can't see." She held her bag up to her chin, imitating that famous scene from *The Sixth Sense*, and whispered dramatically, "I see dead people."

Then she burst out laughing at her own joke, as did Ryan.

"I thought that would make you laugh, too," she said.

"It did," he said as he turned to look at her.

"Thank you, Ryan. I like talking to you. You make me feel heard."

"I like the sound of your voice. You have a way of explaining things that makes sense to me." Ryan met her gaze with a steady look. "I'm serious," he said. "Your voice is calming, and I like it."

Their eyes locked, the silence between them thick with anticipation. Emma nervously tucked a strand of hair behind her ear, her pulse quickening. Ryan ran his hand through his hair, clearly feeling the weight of the moment. They began to lean in, their lips almost meeting when the train's door dinged open.

"34th Street, Penn Station," the announcement blared, jolting them out of their moment.

Ryan exhaled sharply and pulled back.

"We better hurry," he said, casting her a quick smile and adjusting the bag on his shoulder.

Emma let out a soft breath. Without another word, they stepped off the train, the near kiss still lingering in the air between them.

CHAPTER 16

SPIRIT OF COMPASSION

Emma and Ryan were caught in a sea of people rushing up the stairs as they stepped off the train. Emma's attention was immediately drawn to a woman carrying a baby wrapped tightly in her arms. The sight was eerily familiar, as it was the same woman and child she had seen in her vision earlier.

"Give me the formula," Emma said to Ryan, her voice firm with purpose.

Ryan handed over the bag from the bodega, and Emma took it gratefully. She approached the woman and offered her the bag with a warm, reassuring smile. "You need this to feed your baby." She placed her hand gently yet knowingly on the woman.

The woman looked at her, momentarily stunned. She gripped Emma's hand tightly as her face lit up with relief and gratitude. "I prayed to God for somebody to help us, and He answered my prayers with you. Thank you."

Emma took her hand away as the woman clutched the bag, her eyes brimming with tears of thanks. "Go see Father Williams at Our Lady of Sorrows Roman Catholic Church in Corona,

Queens. He will help you and your baby. You'll be in expert hands."

The woman nodded and walked away, and Emma turned to see Ryan's reaction. He looked as though he was grappling with the reality of what he had just seen, something so outside the ordinary that it was almost incomprehensible.

Ryan finally broke the silence, his voice filled with curiosity. "So that's why you wanted the formula and water."

Emma met his gaze, her expression softening with a mix of reassurance and understanding. "Yes. I had a vision this morning. I saw the woman and her hungry baby."

She noticed the deep contemplation in his eyes as he tried to piece together the extraordinary scene he had just witnessed. It was clear that this moment had struck a chord with him, shifting his perspective on what was possible.

Emma's heart fluttered slightly at the thought of how this experience might have opened a new door for Ryan that could lead him to a deeper understanding of the world she navigated daily.

As they ascended the stairs from the bustling subway station, the air between them seemed charged with unresolved questions. Ryan's expression remained thoughtful, clearly wrestling with his newfound understanding. He turned to Emma, curiosity, and a hint of frustration evident in his gaze. "You could have told me," he said.

Emma paused, "I told you I'm not forthcoming. Protective. That I don't easily share every detail of my visions or reveal that I'm a psychic medium. I'm sorry if it seemed misleading."

A whirlwind of emotions swirled within her, regret for being afraid to be more open, frustration at not being understood in the past, and vulnerability from sharing her true self.

Emma stopped walking as they reached the corner. She turned to face Ryan, her gaze searching his for any clue to his thoughts.

The bustling street around them seemed to fade as she focused on his expression, hoping to understand his reaction to their earlier conversation.

"Is my gift and my apprehension about it a problem for you?" she asked, her words trembling slightly. This was the moment that could change everything between them.

Ryan's eyes softened with a mix of admiration and uncertainty. He took a deep breath, holding her gaze. "No," he said slowly, his voice steady but tinged with hesitation. "It's not a problem. But it's a lot to process."

Emma's breath caught, her hope mingling with fear. The hesitation in his voice was louder than any outright rejection, leaving her to grapple with the potential fallout of their conversation.

She looked away and continued across the street toward her phone provider.

Ryan glanced at Emma, a thoughtful expression on his face. "You know," he began, his tone firm and genuine, "even though I might not fully understand your abilities, I see that your desire to help people is just as strong as mine."

Emma looked at him, her curiosity piqued.

"I became an orthopedic doctor because I wanted to help people by fixing their bones and improving their mobility," Ryan explained. "And from what I've seen, you're doing the same fixing with your unique gifts. We might come from different worlds, my world of science and yours of spirituality, but our goals are aligned. You're reaching out to help people with your abilities, just as I do with medicine."

Emma's eyes softened, touched by his words. "I appreciate that, Ryan. It means a lot to hear you say that."

Ryan gave her a reassuring smile. "It's the truth. We're different, but we complement each other perfectly in many ways." He stopped walking. So did she.

Their faces drew closer, the magnetic pull between them growing stronger. Emma's breath hitched as she felt Ryan step closer, his body so near, their eyes locked in an intense gaze. The bustling street seemed to blur around them, their focus narrowing to the moment they were about to share.

Just as the world felt like it was closing in on their intimate moment, the blaring horn of a bus pierced the air behind them. The sudden, jarring noise jolted them back to reality, and they both stepped back, their faces flush with the interruption.

Laughter burst forth from them, a mix of surprise and nervousness escaping into the air. Their hands, which had been entwined, now separated as they moved on.

Their laughter gradually faded as they regained their composure. Together, they walked toward the cellular provider store a block from Macy's, the earlier moment still hanging in the air between them. Their blossoming romance added an air of exhilaration to their every step.

CHAPTER 17

WEDDING GIFT

After dropping off Emma's phone at the provider, Ryan and Emma entered Macy's elevators and traveled to the ninth floor for the wedding registry.

Emma walked to the china section while Ryan was checking the registry with a saleswoman. She stopped, struck by a set of Lenox plates decorated with exquisitely detailed butterflies.

Ryan joined her.

"Oh, my goodness, look at these." She breathed, captivated by their beauty. "Aren't they just beautiful?" She felt an inner voice urging her to buy them.

Ryan said, "They remind me of our mother. She decorated our apartment with butterfly motifs everywhere," he said.

"Do you think she would like them?" Emma asked.

"I do, but I just ordered the glassware. We need to find Mia."

When Ryan stepped off the escalator on the fifth floor, he could not believe the sheer size of the flagship store, with an endless array of dresses as far as the eye could see.

He glanced around but saw no sign of Mia." I don't see

her," he said to Emma. He was about to go another direction when he heard a faint scream down the aisle.

Instantly recognizing her voice, Ryan spun around and saw Mia standing among the creamy white gowns, looking up at him with the biggest smile. They rushed toward each other and embraced tightly.

Ryan pulled away, remembering Emma. He gestured for her to come closer and said, "Mia, I'd like you to meet Emma."

Mia stepped back and obviously studied her from head to toe before offering her hand in greeting. "Nice to meet you," she said with a warm smile.

Emma shook Mia's hand gently and replied, "You, too."

Mia looked at Ryan and Emma with wide eyes, excitement and anxiety bubbling over. "I'm trying to find a dress for my wedding on Saturday," she said, her voice a mix of eagerness and stress. "Formal wear isn't my thing, but, you know, when you're getting married, you must go all out. It's just a lot to take in!"

Ryan knew that she wanted his opinion, as she looked at him with both hope and vulnerability. Since their mother had passed away, Ryan and his sister were close. Their family included aunts, uncles, and cousins, but he tried to be her anchor, the one who truly understood her despite the challenges they faced together.

Mia glanced around the store, her eyes drawn to a striking dress. After a moment of consideration, she grabbed another two dresses and a beaded one.

"Emma," Mia said quietly as she held up the dresses, "what do you think? I could use another woman's advice."

"They're lovely, "Emma said. "Which one do you like better?"

"I am not sure," Mia said. "Let me try them on, and you

and Ryan can help me decide," she added with a wink toward Ryan. And Mia went into a fitting room.

When she stepped out of the changing area wearing a strapless mermaid gown, Emma gasped at how tight the dress was on Mia.

With an arched eyebrow, she asked, "Mia...do you think you'll be comfortable with that?"

Ryan, clearly out of his element with fashion, said, "I think it looks great on you."

Mia looked at herself in the mirror and shook her head. "No, I don't feel comfortable in this one," she said, turning toward Emma. "I'll try on another one."

Emma gave a reassuring smile.

When Mia next stepped out of the dressing room, she was wearing the heavily beaded gown.

Ryan glanced at it and said, "I think I like the first one better."

Emma studied Mia closely, noting how the heavy fabric strained her delicate shoulders. "Girl," she said. "You don't look comfortable, and you're having difficulty walking. What style of dresses do you usually wear? Maybe we can help you find something that will look good on you and make you feel good, too."

"I want a long, simple gown," she said, her gaze steady. "No lace, nothing too fancy. I just want it to be elegant and true to who I am."

"Let me see what I can find." Emma offered a supportive smile and set out to find the perfect dress.

As Ryan watched his sister and Emma search for the ideal gown, he stood up to help.

"What about this one?" he suggested, pointing at a dress decorated with sparkling sequins.

To which both Mia and Emma simultaneously replied with a resolute, "No!"

Suddenly, Emma's gaze fell on a stunning satin mermaid dress, a perfect blend of elegance and simplicity. It featured a sweetheart neckline and a sleek, streamlined silhouette with no lace or frills. The dress was understated yet captivating, and Mia's eyes sparkled with excitement as she eagerly agreed to try it on.

Emma beamed with pride as Mia cautiously stepped out of the dressing room wearing the dress. "You look gorgeous!" she exclaimed.

Ryan smiled at his sister and uttered, "Mom would cry right now, Mia. You look stunning. No joke." Mia walked to the mirror, her dark brown hair swept up with a clip, her hazel eyes sparkling with delight.

Mia looked into the mirror. "I can't believe it! It's perfect!" She turned to. "Thank you both."

Mia approached the checkout counter, her face glowing with excitement. Emma couldn't help but notice the subtle undercurrent between Ryan and his sister. Having observed him for a while, she sensed that he was genuinely pleased to be there with Mia. She also felt a faint connection between them, hinting that her own feelings for Ryan might not have gone unnoticed. Emma hoped that this special moment was the beginning of something meaningful.

Her curiosity piqued, she asked, "Would you two like to grab a coffee?" She was eager for more time together to uncover what was unfolding between them.

"Yes," they said in unison and headed for a nearby Starbucks. They approached the coffee counter, and Ryan gave the barista their orders. The barista gave them all a polite smile, but

Emma could swear that the barista kept her gaze on him longer than necessary as she kept smiling at him and blushing.

They took their coffees and found a table.

"I can't stay long," Emma said. "I'm waiting for a call from the phone repair shop. They'll contact Ryan when it is ready."

Mia leaned in. "So, how did you two actually meet?"

Emma took a breath. "Okay, the real reason? I have a mild concussion. Someone shoved me into a beam on the subway."

Mia's smile vanished. "Wait, seriously? You got hurt?"

Emma nodded. "Yes. I ran into Ryan at Penn Station not long after. I had a pounding headache, and he offered me a place to stay."

Mia's eyes moved between them. "That sounds like my brother. Always the doctor helping someone in need."

Ryan looked over at Mia, and they exchanged a brief, quiet glance.

Mia raised an eyebrow. "You accepted an offer from a stranger?"

Emma held her coffee cup and took a nervous sip. "I know how it sounds. But my phone was completely wrecked, I was disoriented, and he felt safe. My intuition told me I could trust him."

Ryan spoke calmly. "She needed help. And I know her doctor, Justin, the one who treated her."

Emma paused, choosing her words carefully. "Sometimes, I get these strong feelings or signs that guide me. I agreed because of a mix of intuition and a little sign. I saw a white feather falling from the sky. The feather was like the heavens telling me to say yes. I knew then that I had to accept. It was as if something greater than myself wanted me to go with him."

Mia paused for a moment to take in the information. "My brother is a good guy."

"Yes, he is, "Emma agreed, and they both looked at Ryan, who sat there looking a little embarrassed.

Emma looked up and saw Luna standing nearby, watching her children with a quiet look of pride.

"So, you eloped?" Emma asked, changing the subject.

Mia nodded. "Jacob and I didn't want to go through the hassle of a wedding ceremony," she began. "We wanted to save that money for a house. We ended up going down to Queens Boulevard Courthouse and getting married there. Easy-peasy. But after our families found out, we realized they felt left out of our day."

At this moment, Luna's voice, though gentle and other-worldly, reached Emma. "Ask her about the butterfly."

"Do you remember seeing a butterfly?" Emma asked.

Mia paused, her forehead wrinkling. "Yes, I did. When we left the courthouse. I remember because it reminded me of my mother."

"There were butterflies all over our apartment. Our mother loved them," Ryan said.

"Yes," Mia said.

Emma's gaze became distant for a moment, as if she were listening to something beyond the visible world. The scene subtly shifted, and for a brief instant, Luna's ethereal presence became tangible. Luna, Mia's mother, stood beside her daughter and next to her son, and a gentle, comforting aura surrounded her. She appeared as a soft, shimmering figure, her features tender and serene.

Emma's voice softened as she spoke. "It was your mother, Mia, letting you know she was spiritually with you."

Mia's expression was doubtful, her gaze darting around as if trying to catch a glimpse of her mother's spirit. "You really think that was her?" she asked, her voice trembling with a mixture of awe and hope.

Ryan watched his sister with concern. He placed a hand on hers.

"Yes," Emma said, her gaze still on Luna. "Sometimes, those we love find ways to reach out and let us know they're watching."

Mia blinked in surprise while Ryan shivered, getting more accustomed to these supernatural occurrences.

Mia whispered, "My mother?"

"Your mom is here today." Then she tried to explain. "I am a psychic medium. I can connect to those who have passed."

Mia teared up as she heard this. On the other side of her, Ryan looked away, as if to hide his own emotions.

"Your mother loves you and your new husband, Jacob," Emma continued, "and she was there with you on that day at the courthouse. The white butterfly was her."

Luna's spirit hovered nearby, a gentle, shimmering presence. Emma could feel her reassuring essence and see the faint outline of her figure like a delicate, radiant mist. Luna's voice was clear and soothing, a whisper in Emma's mind that conveyed the depth of a mother's love.

"She wants you to know," Emma said, her tone light and filled with affection, "that even when you become pregnant, she will be watching over you and her grandbaby. She says it should be arriving very soon."

Mia's hand flew to her mouth in surprise, and a smile began to spread across her face.

"But how does she know?" Mia's voice trembled with wonder as she absorbed the revelation.

"From her place in heaven, where she can see everything bathed in love and light, she's been holding her grandbaby in spirit, who is with her until it's time to enter your life."

"Thank you, Emma," Mia said quietly, her voice thick with emotion. "That means more to me than you could ever know."

Emma reached out and gently touched Mia, her own heart full. "You're welcome. I'm glad I could help you feel closer to her, to speak for her."

Ryan watched the exchange with a mixture of awe and curiosity. The depth of the connection between Mia and their mother and Emma's role in bridging that gap left him deeply moved.

"Wow, you just gave us a mic drop moment," Mia said, then laughed.

Just then, Ryan's phone rang. He answered, then hung up. "Your phone is ready to be picked up."

"Awesome," Emma said and stood up as Ryan did the same.

Mia hugged her and said, "You have to come to my wedding this Saturday." She turned to her brother. "Ryan, you have to bring her."

He laughed. "You heard her, Emma, I can't let my sister down."

Emma smiled, feeling her face flush at Ryan's words. "I wouldn't miss it, Mia." Turning toward Ryan, she added, "I guess we'll see each other soon." And she walked toward the phone provider.

Mia turned to Ryan and said, "Wow!" she exclaimed. "Where did you find her?"

He watched Emma walk away, his gaze soft and affectionate.

"Almost from the moment I met her, I felt an immediate sense of comfort and ease with her. A connection."

"She's someone you naturally feel at home with. Kind. She is so easy to talk to."

"I know what you mean about her," he said, his voice carrying a hint of admiration. "We talked all night, and I lost track of time."

Ryan saw Mia's gaze sharpened as she studied him. "Do you believe her? Could she really be seeing this?"

"I do," Ryan said. "She is special."

Mia realized it was as if everything had suddenly come into focus. Ryan was falling in love! He might not have realized it himself yet, but she could see it clearly in the way her brother looked at Emma. "Something special is blooming between you. Think you are falling for her. I saw how you watch her, Ryan."

He said nothing, but Emma was in his thoughts the way no one had been before. He wasn't willing to tell his sister anything. It felt too new to believe. "I need to get going."

He said goodbye with a brotherly kiss. He watched Mia head off to her husband, and he left for home.

CHAPTER 18

PHONE ISSUES & EPIPHANY

Emma descended the escalator and headed toward Macy's wedding registry to purchase the Lenox butterfly plates. She wanted them to be delivered quickly.

As Emma was leaving Macy's, she paused at the sparkling jewelry counter when she saw a beautiful necklace with angel wings. When the salesgirl took it out of the case, Emma felt a strange sense of connection with it. It was as if the necklace were speaking to her, telling her to buy it.

Emma knew she had to get home, but she followed her instincts and purchased the beautiful necklace. After paying for it, she carefully placed it around her neck and instantly felt comforted. Given everything that had happened to her, it was as if the necklace were a guardian angel watching over her, which she felt she needed right now.

Outside Macy's, the cool air hit her as she approached the glass-fronted mobile phone store, its bright interior gleaming under fluorescent lights. Inside, customers milled around, tapping on display phones while techs in branded shirts assisted them. Emma approached the counter, only to find out that they couldn't access her old phone's data. She let out a sigh of frustration as she paid for her new phone.

A feeling of helplessness grew inside her as she powered on the new phone and began setting up her passcode.The shiny screen reflected her frustrated expression.

"Great," she muttered under her breath, resigned to the fact that there was a long shot that her contacts were backed up somewhere. She would have to try her luck with her laptop later.

Maybe this whole mess was more than just bad luck with a broken phone. It felt as though something beyond her control was preventing her from returning home.

A few minutes later pocketed the receipt and headed for the exit. The bell above the door chimed softly as she stepped back into the bustling street. She stopped. She couldn't go home. Where was home?

Oh snap, she forgot the Post-it that Gary gave her. She reached into her jeans pocket, and it was empty.

Emma's heart skipped a beat as panic set in.

This was great. The one thing that could help get her home was gone. She racked her brain, trying to remember which police station her sister and Gary worked out of. Why was it so impossible to recall?

She made a quick decision. Since the officer took her ID and she couldn't remember her address, she headed toward Penn Station to see if the same police officers were there or if one could help her find a police officer who took her driver's license.

When Emma felt frustrated, usually she would take a deep breath and center herself, trusting in the guidance she always felt from the divine. But this was unlike anything she had experienced before. Her mind was spinning with gaps she couldn't fill. She couldn't remember her home, her parents, or even how to reach her sister. And worse yet, she hadn't even thought to get Ryan's phone number.

"Seriously Emma?" she muttered under her breath, shaking her head.

How could I forget something so simple?

She kicked a small pebble on the sidewalk, watching it skidded away. Her stomach tightened. She had a knot of anxiety she wasn't used to feeling. She was normally so composed, but today, the sense of calm she relied on was nowhere to be found.

"Come on, Emma," she whispered to herself. "You've dealt with far worse than this. You see dead people for crying out loud. You can handle this." But even as she tried to reassure herself, she couldn't shake the nagging feeling that without that note, she was utterly lost.

Emma pushed through the heavy glass door of Penn Station, the rush of cool air meeting her as she entered. She scanned the bustling station, and she saw a large, marked sign that read, NYPD Transit District 4.

She navigated through the crowd until she reached the police desk where a uniformed officer was busy with paperwork.

"How can I help you?" the desk officer asked.

"I was in an incident yesterday and taken to the hospital," Emma explained. "I believe the officer who responded still has my ID. It wasn't with my belongings."

The officer inquired, "What's your name?"

"Emma Duque."

The officer searched the system and saw that someone had called about the ID earlier that day. "The notes indicate that it was given to Officer Gary Walters."

Gary must have thought he was doing her a favor by picking

it up. Emma paused, frustrated, then asked, "Can you give me my home address?"

The officer seemed unsettled by the question. "You don't know where you live?" he asked, his tone a mix of curiosity and suspicion.

Emma tried to explain, "He took my ID, and I just need the address on it."

The officer's expression softened slightly, but he still seemed firm. "I wasn't on duty when Officer Walters came by, and under privacy laws, I'm not able to give out any personal information, including addresses. You'll need to contact Officer Walters directly for that."

Emma pressed, "Can you at least give me his contact information?"

The officer shook his head. "I don't have that either. If you're finished here, there are three people waiting behind you."

Turning around, she noticed another person had joined the line, making it four people now. With a frustrated sigh, she turned and walked away, understanding he wasn't going to help her.

Emma exited the Penn Station police office. Her mind was a whirlwind of confusion and urgency. Her ID had already been given to Gary, but she felt lost with no way to contact him. Without her old phone, she had no contacts or access to her social media. She had no clue how to get home, and her hospital papers only provided her date of birth and medical records number, offering no help.

Reluctantly, she gave up and made her way back upstairs to the bustling street. The sounds of honking cars and chattering pedestrians filled the air as she emerged from the subway station, feeling defeated and overwhelmed. As she stepped onto the sidewalk, a wave of frustration and despair washed over her. Tears welled up in her eyes, and she struggled to contain her emotions as she tried to find of her elusive memories.

The blur of yellow taxis, bustling pedestrians, and dizzying lights surrounded her. She tried to hold herself together as she walked.

Emma Moment: *It feels like something is against me, like when you miss the bus by just a few seconds, or when you prepare for an outdoor event and it starts pouring rain as soon as you step outside.*

She felt alone as she walked down one block and then another, her thoughts turned to her sister and how fortunate she was that her life seemed so stable. Despite her happiness for her sister's upcoming wedding, Emma couldn't help but feel a pang of envy. She wondered why finding a meaningful relationship had been so elusive for her. Sometimes she felt adrift, struggling to understand her own mission of helping others, especially since her visions and dreams seemed to guide her in different directions. Given her recent concussion, the confusion and uncertainty felt even more overwhelming.

Suddenly, she felt a chill as dark clouds blotted out the sun, casting an eerie shadow over the city. There St. Patrick's Cathedral towered above the other buildings nearby, sending shivers down her spine.

Inside, the interior of St. Patrick's Cathedral was serene, with the soft echoes of prayers reverberating through the majestic space. As Emma moved through the aisles, she accidentally bumped into a small table covered with pamphlets. The table wobbled, sending a few pamphlets fluttering to the floor.

A young boy, who had been standing too close to the table, stumbled and fell.

Emma's concern quickly shifted into action. She bent down to help him. "I'm so sorry," she said, her voice filled with worry.

The boy looked up at her, his eyes wide with astonishment.

"You can see me?" he asked, his voice carrying a note of surprise.

Emma paused, her heart racing. Though she had encountered spirits like Luna, her mind, clouded by worry and her recent concussion, didn't immediately register the boy as a spirit. The boy's appearance seemed ordinary at first glance. Only when she took a closer look did she notice subtle signs that didn't quite fit. His form seemed slightly blurred around the edges.

"Yes, I can see you," Emma said.

"My name is Lucas," he told her.

Emma sat in a nearby pew. "Come, sit by me."

The boy sat next to her and said, "I've been following my mommy, and she likes to come to this church. I've been trying to talk to her, but she cannot hear me."

Emma listened intently, and her heart broke for the little boy. "What do you want to tell your mom?"

"I want my mommy to know I am okay; it was not her fault. I ran after my ball into the street," Lucas explained. She cries all the time. I wish I had angel wings to give her."

At the boy's words, she touched the angel necklace she had been compelled to buy. "Lucas, do you see your mom here?" Emma asked.

"Yes, that's her." He pointed to a woman kneeling at the end of the next aisle.

"Come with me, and we can go to her together." She took

his hand, and they walked to where his mother was praying. Emma let Lucas go first and sat beside him. She took a deep breath and said quietly, "I'm unsure how to start this, but I am a psychic medium. Do you know what that means?"

"I do not have any money, and I do not believe in ghosts," the woman said, returning to her rosary.

"I have something to tell you. I just bumped into a little boy, and he told me his name is Lucas. He said he has been trying to talk to you, but you cannot hear him."

The woman's eyes started to water, and tears rolled down her face. "My baby Lucas is not here anymore. I feel so empty inside."

Lucas placed his tiny hands on his mother's hand, and she looked astonished. "Lucas, is that you?" she asked, feeling his little hands on her.

Lucas looked at Emma. "Can you tell my mommy not to cry anymore? I am okay, and I'm with Grandma."

"Lucas is here. He wants you to know he is okay and is with Grandma." She looked at Lucas' mother with gentle reassurance.

The woman's eyes widened, and she looked down at her hand, where her son's was touching hers. "Lucas," she whispered.

"I can see an older woman named Delores waiting for Lucas," Emma told her.

"Oh," the woman said, "my mother was Delores. Lucas's grandmother. She died before he was born. How could you know that?"

Emma removed the necklace from her neck and placed it in Matilda's hand. "Lucas wants you to have this. He wants to give you angel wings, so you will know you are not alone, and he will visit you. But you must stop feeling guilty because you could not have done anything to stop what happened."

The woman lifted the necklace and looked at it. Lucas's small hands moved the wings back and forth, making the necklace shimmer.

"Is that you moving the wings, Lucas?" she asked, her voice trembling.

The wings fluttered more vigorously, and Lucas's voice, full of excitement, echoed in her mind. "My mommy can see me! Mommy, I will be your little angel watching over you. I love you."

"I love you, my son, and I will wear this to keep you with me always."

Lucas stood up and stopped in front of his mom, kissing her on the cheeks. His mother brought her hand to her cheeks, feeling his butterfly kisses.

Lucas walked to the cathedral doors, where the woman Delores was waiting. He reached up and took her hand, and they began to walk away. But he turned back, blew a kiss to Emma, and said, "Thank you."

Emma wiped away her tears. "He is gone."

His mother grabbed Emma and engulfed her in a hug. Both women clung to each other for the miracles they had received.

Emma felt the love and energy in that church.

His mother said, "Thank you. I have never believed in psychic mediums before, but I do now. This is a day that I will never forget. My Lucas is gone, but I know he is not alone. He is with my mother. I do not feel the overwhelming sadness I felt when I walked in today."

Emma smiled at her through the tears and said, "I'm happy you could feel him here today, and I can tell you that you will, from time to time, know when he is around you. You have been given a great gift today."

Matilda rose and asked, "Who are you?"

"I am Emma Duque."

"I am Matilda,"

Emma rose and gave Matilda her business card. "You can call me anytime you want to talk. It doesn't matter what time."

Emma watched Matilda leave and went to sit in the front pews. She lowered to the bench, knelt, and began to pray. "Dear Father, thank you for letting me see the hope I could give Matilda, who thought she had lost everything, and for letting me help little Lucas reunite with his mom and grandma and bring him home to you.

"Father, forgive me for being selfish and thinking only of myself. Please help me," she whispered. "I am so lost. If it is your will, lift this fog from my mind." She paused. "Amen."

A deep voice reverberated around her. "My child," the voice said. "Why have you come here today?"

Emma turned around, but there was no one in sight. Goosebumps ran down her arms. She made the sign of the cross and moved back onto the pew. Shaken.

"Hello, Emma. May I sit here?" Emma heard a voice say.

Standing next to her was a nun, who stared at Emma with knowing eyes that seemed to peer into her soul.

"Yes," Emma muttered, swallowing the lump in her throat and moving aside so the nun could sit.

The nun raised an eyebrow and sat beside her, not saying a word.

They sat in silence until Emma finally glanced at the nun. To her astonishment, the nun's face began to change, morphing into the familiar face of Angel.

"Angel!" Emma exclaimed in recognition, a wave of joy surging through her. All her worries melted away as she sighed with relief, thanking God under her breath.

Without wasting a moment, the nun turned toward Emma and spoke. "My child, I have come as you requested."

For a moment, Emma still felt disoriented and confused. She gazed at the nun before asking, "Why can't I remember where I live or where my parents live?"

Angel replied with her kind yet deep eyes, reflecting every emotion in Emma's heart. "Things are happening the way they are supposed to, Emma."

Emma Moment: *We all have contracts that detail everything we will do on Earth, our purpose, written in the Akashic records. Everyone has one, even animals.*

Emma said, "I am lost and overwhelmed and do not know what to do."

Angel squeezed her hand and replied, "Everything will become clear to you soon. You need to return to Ryan's home for now."

Emma shook her head again and said, "I told them it would only be for the night. If I return now, they will think I lost it. I can't go back."

Angel smiled gently at Emma. "The family is expecting you. Did you check your bag? You left your laptop."

Emma quickly opened her weekend bag and, sure enough, found that her laptop was missing.

Angel's expression softened as she tenderly continued, "Just go back, and everything will unfold as it should. Remember, there's a lesson here that you've been avoiding, but you must learn it. I tell you, you've already learned part of it. You are never alone, my child. Have faith and know that all will be revealed in its own time."

After taking a few deep breaths to calm herself, Emma felt a calmness wrap around her. She closed her eyes, settling into the peace she felt.

When she opened her eyes again, she had no idea how much time had passed, minutes or hours. She turned to look at Angel, ready to express her gratitude, but Angel was gone. There was no nun.

Emma looked around. The church was not as full as when she sat down. Had she fallen asleep? How much time had passed?

She scrambled up and rushed out of the church. Outside, the streets were filled with commuters going home, and the sun was no longer visible in the skyline. She had lost hours. She rushed to catch the train back to Ryan's home in the Bronx. She was both worried and distressed because this was something she had never experienced before, and she didn't know what to expect. Despite her anxiety, she trusted Angel to guide her correctly.

Emma knew she had told Ryan's family that she would only be spending the night. But Angel had said they expected her. What would happen if she showed up there? She hurried to catch the right train and as it pulled away from the platform, Emma looked out the window, watching the white subway tiles flash by, and the surroundings went dark. She wondered how she had managed to leave her laptop behind. She didn't even remember taking it out.

CHAPTER 19

RETURNING TO FATE

Emma's heart raced nervously as she approached the front door of Ryan's home. She was not sure what kind of reception she would receive, but she knew she had to trust what Angel had told her. As she raised her hand to knock, the door let out a loud creak and swung open, revealing Alex on the other side. His warm hazel eyes lit up at the sight of her, his lips curving into a welcoming smile that reached all the way to his dimpled cheeks.

"Ah! There you are," he said, taking in a deep breath of fresh air. "We've been waiting for you. My mom is in the kitchen. Go on in."

Alex moved aside before resuming his task of taking out the garbage.

Emma said as she stepped into the kitchen, which had various bubbling pots and pans on the stove. "Hi."

Anne looked up from the stove and replied, "Oh good. There you are."

"Hi," Alyssa said.

Emma then continued, "I'm so sorry, but I think I need to stay another night."

Alyssa glanced up from the counter. She laughed and said, "You sure are a funny lady!"

Emma frowned. "Why do you say that?"

"Yesterday, you told everyone you'd be staying until Sunday," Alyssa replied with a grin. "That's when your parents are expected to return."

"I did? I'm sorry. My head still isn't right. Lingering effects of a concussion, I guess," she said, her face brightening.

Emma Moment: *It's like I'm in a scene from Men in Black, where they erase your memory. But this is divine intervention. I realize now why we sometimes forget things when we walk into another room.*

"Dad and Ryan are in the backyard, cooking dinner and getting it ready for tomorrow's wedding. You do remember it's tomorrow, right?" Alyssa said.

Anne interjected gently, "Now, now, be nice. Sorry, Emma, she can be too outspoken."

"Yes, I do remember. Thanks," Emma said with a grin. She told Anne she was going to freshen up and would be back to help with dinner.

"Take your time. Theo is grilling, so we are all set. All you need to do is go outside and eat," Anne said with a smile.

Emma opened the bedroom door, dropped off her bag, washed up, and made her way out to the backyard.

Outside, she was stunned by the yard's transformation, taking in the backyard with its flowers and LED string lights illuminating the space. The tables and chairs were all arranged, and there was even a spot off to the side, under the covered porch, for a DJ.

Theo looked up and called out, "Come here, Emma! Get a plate, help yourself. We've got plenty of BBQ ribs."

"Hi, Emma, have a seat," Ryan said, pulling out a chair for her and offering her a charming smile.

Emma felt her cheeks flush, and a swarm of butterflies danced merrily in her stomach as she took her seat. When Ryan settled back into his chair beside her, she noticed a smear of BBQ sauce across his cheek.

Emma handed him a napkin. "You have BBQ sauce on your face."

He took it, and their fingers brushed. She felt a spark of something electric between them. He looked down at the smear of sauce on his hand, then up at her with a crooked smile. "Be right back. Gonna wash this off."

He didn't wait for a reply, just winked and walked off, leaving her somewhere between amused and flustered.

Just as Ryan entered the house, Anne emerged with a plate of corn and potatoes for Emma. Theo, Anne, and the kids had already eaten, having enjoyed their meal earlier in the backyard. Because it was game night for the family."

Anne set down the platter and Emma helped herself. She looked up from her corn and said, "I met Mia today, and Ryan and I helped her choose a dress for the wedding. She invited me to the ceremony and reception."

Theo turned away from cleaning off the BBQ. "You'll be joining us for the after-party, too, since you're staying here until Sunday."

"Yes," she said after a moment of thought. "I'd love to."

He then headed back inside to prepare the game table for a fun night of old shows and UNO.

Anne told her, "Ryan should be back soon. I'm going to check on Matthew. The doctor said he had a virus and to keep him hydrated with lots of liquids."

"I will pray for him to get better before I go to bed tonight," Emma said.

"Go ahead and eat, and then come inside. We will be in the living room.

Her stomach grumbled. She had not thought about food since grabbing that coffee and muffin at Macy's. Emma took her first bite of the corn on the cob, which was so good. Just the right amount of butter and salt, and the ribs were messy but wonderful.

Ryan walked out to the backyard, his pace quickening as he neared Emma. Alyssa followed him, heading for the dirty dishes by the grill. His face softened with a pleased look as his gaze met Emma. "Hey," he said, trying to sound casual. He grabbed a napkin, dipped it in a nearby cup of water, cleared his throat, and gently wiped away the spot of BBQ sauce from her cheek.

"Looks like the tables have turned," she said with a laugh. Emma was struck by an unexpected yearning to be near him. She was unsure whether her feelings were echoing in her mind or if she had spoken to them aloud. The distinction was blurred for her.

Emma looked up. Her gaze fell upon Ryan's mesmerizing features, illuminated by the bright moonlight. She found herself engulfed by a rush of joy, anxiety, and longing, her heart pounding and her breath catching in her throat. The intensity of her feelings was so overwhelming that it manifested physically. An unexpected rush of emotion caused her to choke slightly on her food, her eyes welling up with tears that she struggled to hold back.

She let out a series of painful coughs. In an instant, Ryan was already patting her back and handing her a glass of icy water, which she sipped slowly. That did the trick.

Wiping her mouth and cheeks with the damp napkin, she gave him a small smile through teary eyes. "We're even now," she whispered softly.

Alyssa spelled out, "K-I-S-S-I-N-G!" as she walked past them, heading inside. They had both forgotten she was even there.

The heat between them was palpable as Ryan leaned in closer, his warm breath fanning her face and his intense gaze sweeping over every feature of hers. She felt her worries dissipating in his presence. She felt lost in this tender moment of romance as each of them allowed their feelings to unite and take part in something beautiful.

Ryan's heart raced as he drew closer to Emma. He studied her delicate features in the moonlight, illuminated like a divine being. She sat there looking up into the night sky, and her beauty took his breath away. "It's a beautiful night."

"Emma," Ryan breathed. "I've been thinking about you all day."

"You have?"

"I have."

A faint blush came to her cheeks as she replied, "I enjoyed getting to know your sister, Mia."

"Mia is also very excited to see you again," Ryan said.

Suddenly wordless, they both looked up at the multitude of stars above them, a shooting star streaked across the night sky.

In unison, they exclaimed, "Make a wish!"

"But do not tell me what it is," Ryan said. "Otherwise, it won't come true."

Ryan closed his eyes and made his wish, while Emma, caught up in the magic of the moment, wished to hold onto the clarity of their connection, hoping it would anchor her to the present and help her remember this fleeting, perfect moment.

CHAPTER 20

INTERRUPTIONS

Emma and Ryan were still under their connection spell when they went inside, where the family was in the living room, gathered around the TV watching *I Love Lucy*.

Laughter filled the room. Ryan and Emma sat on the loveseat, and Theo, Anne, Alyssa, and Alex giggled on the nearby sofa.

"I feel like a kid again," Emma exclaimed. "I used to watch this with my family."

After a few minutes, Emma rested her head on Ryan's shoulder. Ryan looked down at her with a warm smile and slipped his arm around her. The simple gesture brought a profound sense of security and closeness she hadn't anticipated, but it felt incredibly right. They sat there together, Emma savoring the moment and reluctant to move.

Ryan's mind raced with a flurry of thoughts. He was captivated by her presence. He wanted to understand what made her laugh, what her favorite books and movies were, and how she felt about the little things in life. What were her dreams? What were the moments that shaped her into the person she is today?

All the puzzle pieces fell into place to make Emma the woman she was, the woman he wanted.

Emma felt a familiar, tingling sensation begin to wash over her. Her vision blurred slightly, and a soft, echoing hum filled her ears, signaling that a vision was about to unfold. She felt a growing sense of urgency. Her heart began pounding as if trying to keep pace with the images forming in her mind.

She abruptly sat up. With a quick apology, she headed toward the bathroom to find a quiet space where she could privately fully immerse herself in the vision.

The vision began to unfold, with all its warning of trouble.

When it was over, Emma paused for a moment, then reached for her phone. Her fingers moved quickly over the keypad as if they knew what she needed and how to reach Jack at the radio station where he worked.

Jack. There was no foggy memory loss. Jack was her friend. He owed a debt of gratitude to Emma and considered her a daughter.

"Hello," Jack answered.

"Hi, Jack! It's Emma. I need a last-minute favor. There is a party tomorrow night. I need a speaker with lights and Wi-Fi for the night."

"I can do better than that. I have a DJ available who could come set up and DJ your party. Two hours outdoors. What do you think?"

"That would be amazing, thank you," she said, and gave him the address.

He laughed on the other side of the phone. "Glad I could help. You know I owe you, Emma."

And they exchanged goodbyes.

Emma Moment: *The bright side of having this gift is that, even though it sometimes feels like a burden, moments like these make it all worthwhile.*

Emma had a vision that the DJ for the party at Theo's canceled. Jack had saved the party. She tucked her phone away and paused, already lost in the image of the beautiful music she envisioned filling the outdoor space.

Ryan kept glancing toward the bathroom door, waiting for Emma to return. Anne and Theo sat at the game table and dealt out the Uno cards, their laughter filling the room as they prepared to start the game.

"Hey, Alyssa, ask Ryan to partner with you while I check on your brother," Anne said. "Okay, Mom," Alyssa responded, "Hey, Ryan, do you want to partner with me for this?"

Ryan's gaze was still on the hall where Emma had disappeared.

With a touch of impatience, she snapped her fingers in front of his face. "Ryan, hey! Are you in or out? I need you to team up with me for UNO against Dad and Alex."

Ryan shook his head, then chuckled, feeling slightly embarrassed to have been caught staring after Emma. "Sure, let's do it."

But Ryan saw Emma emerge from behind the door with the most beautiful smile on her face and he froze.

Alyssa, eager to play said to Emma, "Want to partner up with me...girls against the boys?"

"Sure, I'd love to," Emma said, settling into a chair.

Ryan shifted his focus back to the game after hearing the shuffling of cards and hushed whispers from Theo and Alex, who huddled across the table. No doubt they were plotting something nefarious.

"Come on, Emma!" Alyssa implored. "Help me. Let us take these boys down. Girls against the boys."

"You got it," Emma replied with a devious smile as she and Alyssa exchanged a knowing look. "Looks like we girls will have to beat you," Emma remarked, glancing at Theo and Alex.

"Girl's rule; boys drool," Alyssa added with a giggle.

Emma, with a mischievous glint in her eye, placed a card on the table, directing it at Theo. "Red, pick four," she said.

Alyssa played a "Pick 2" red card on Alex, setting off a chain reaction. Alex nonchalantly played "Green 2" in response, provoking simultaneous cries of "Uno!" from Alyssa and Emma.

The tension mounted as Alyssa placed the winning card in a different color, securing a win for the girls. With a triumphant grin, Emma said, "We win!" Alyssa and Emma laughed and exchanged a congratulatory high-five.

While they played, Ryan couldn't help but admire how seamlessly Emma fit in with his family. Emma made everything better. He felt a pang of longing as he watched her laugh and joke with his family. He realized he was falling for her, and it wasn't just about being charmed by her. He imagined sharing more moments like these, building new memories together, and possibly even exploring a future where they could support each other's dreams. The more he saw of her, the more, he felt a growing desire to create something meaningful with her.

Now, as the evening wound down, the girls won the last game, stacking up more wins than the boys, grumbled at they went off to bed.

Tomorrow was Saturday, and the big day, Mia's wedding.

With the street lamp outside casting a soft glow through Ryan's bedroom window, Emma slipped into bed, pulling the covers up to her chin. The anticipation of the next day filled her with a buzz of excitement as she nestled into the warmth and comfort of Ryan's bed, feeling like she was on the brink of something exciting.

Lost in her thoughts, Emma was transported back to her earlier visit with little Lucas at St. Patrick's Cathedral. The memory of the cathedral's serene beauty contrasted sharply with the sudden, jarring reminder of how quickly life can change. The fleeting moments she shared with Lucas, and the realization of how abruptly loved ones can be taken away, washed over her, leaving her with a profound sense of fragility. But even in the face of such heartache, she found comfort in the knowledge that one message of hope could change someone's life.

With a yawn, Emma said a prayer for Matthew, buried her head in her pillow, and drifted easily off to sleep.

CHAPTER 21

WEDDING DAY

Saturday morning, Anne awoke to a message on her cell phone that the DJ they had hired was stuck in Washington, D.C. and had to cancel. She rushed to the kitchen to inform Theo.

"What are we do?" Anne asked, her voice tinged with concern.

Theo shook his head. "Don't worry. I'll ask around and see if anyone has speakers we can borrow."

Theo and Anne were deep in conversation, oblivious to the knock on the door. Alex appeared in the doorway. "Someone's at the door with audio equipment that needs an adult signature." Theo and Anne went to the door where a delivery guy stood with speakers.

"DJ equipment. A wedding gift for the couple," he read from his notes.

Theo and Anne exchanged looks of surprise, shifting from concern to excitement and back to confusion.

"Who sent this?" Anne asked, with a slight shake of her head.

The delivery man shrugged. "Don't know, ma'am. It doesn't say. I'm just the delivery guy. Where do you want me to put it?"

Anne turned to Theo, who stepped forward. "Follow me," he said. He walked out the back door into the backyard with the delivery man.

"Right here is perfect," Theo directed as the delivery guy placed the DJ equipment in the covered lanai.

"Could you sign this form, please?" the delivery guy asked, handing over the document.

Theo signed the delivery form and took the receipt. He gave the delivery man a quick nod and headed back into the kitchen, his mind racing with the implications of the unexpected DJ equipment.

Emma entered the kitchen. "Good morning."

Anne chirped back, "*Buenos días*. It's crazy here today," she laughed.

"Then let me fix breakfast," Emma offered. "Don't say no. I want to help."

Anne agreed, then turned to Theo. "Who could have sent it?"

"I have no idea, but it's exactly what we needed," Theo remarked.

"I'll need some help to set it up and operate it. I'm not exactly familiar with DJ equipment."

Anne reviewed the paperwork. "Theo, it says here that a DJ will be coming to set everything up and handle it all for us."

Theo's face lit up. "Are you serious? That's incredible. We didn't think it was possible to get a full setup like this. Thank you, God," he said, looking out the window at the sky.

Anne nodded. "I can't believe this. We're going to have an amazing party for Mia and Jacob."

Anne and Theo scurried around the kitchen, jotting down notes and checking items off their to-do list. The air was filled with a mix of excitement and nervous energy as they discussed the final touches for the ceremony and reception. Anne had arranged for the cake to be delivered to the church the day before.

Emma retrieved a carton of eggs from the refrigerator. She grabbed a mixing bowl from the cupboard and set about fixing breakfast, and it was going fine until she could not find a sauté pan. It then occurred to her to check the stove, remembering that every Latina knows you can always find pans in the oven. There it was. She laughed to herself, then made scrambled eggs for everyone.

Anne returned to the kitchen, just as Emma had finished the bacon, and she took out the waffles from the freezer and popped them into the toaster.

"Thank you for your help, Emma," Anne said.

"I can't just sit here without lending a hand," Emma said.

Ryan walked into the kitchen with a yawn. "Well, it smells so good. When do we eat?"

Anne took the waffles from the toaster and called out, "Come and eat. Breakfast is ready."

Theo and Alex joined them, clearly hungry. Alyssa slowly shuffled in, wiping her sleepy eyes. "Good morning," she said to everyone.

After giving thanks for their food, Theo began serving up his eggs and said, "Everything is almost ready for the after-party. We need to get to the church before noon."

Without pausing to chew her breakfast, Alyssa piped up and asked Emma, "What color is your dress. Mine is pink."

Emma laughed. "I have a pink dress with flowers on it. We'll both be wearing pink."

Alyssa dove into a detailed description of her outfits. "Oh, wow! I have new pink shoes to wear with my dress. Then, once we returned home, my mom bought me another outfit for the after-party, a matching top and skirt with cute silver shoes. They have low heels." She said excitedly. "My mom bought them for me as a birthday present."

"I remember my first low heels," Emma said, smiling at the memory. "They were white with little bows."

Alex interrupted, "Come on, everybody! If we don't get ready soon, we won't get out the door. Look at the time."

Everyone turned to the clock.

Alyssa suddenly jumped up, put her dishes clattering into the sink, and bolted for her bedroom.

Ryan glanced at Alex in relief. "Thank you," he whispered.

Alex stood up. "I love my sister, but she sometimes talks way too much." He gave them a mischievous grin and headed off to shower and change.

Emma turned to Anne. "You go. I'll clean up. It won't take me long to get ready."

Anne thanked her, and she and Theo excused themselves to get changed.

Ryan wanted a moment alone with Emma before they left. He knew this was the perfect time, with Alyssa's chatter having finally ceased.

His chance to make a move was slipping away. He paused, running his fingers through his brown hair, gathering his courage.

Emma felt her heart skip a beat as he fixated on her with

those intoxicating hazel eyes. A crooked smile appeared on his lips.

"Would you like to ride with me to church? I'll happily take you." His voice was warm and inviting.

She felt the heat rise in her cheeks from his gaze and replied, "It's a date."

He froze momentarily and let out a small chuckle before replying, a devilish smile playing on his lips, "It's a date." With that, he strolled out of the kitchen, whistling an old tune.

Emma smiled as she began loading the dishwasher. What is it about Ryan? He's attractive, with the handsomest hazel eyes. A girl could get used to having those muscular arms around her. She let out a small sigh at the thought.

After finishing the last of the dishes, she headed off to get dressed. Inside the bedroom, she slipped into her flowered dress and took out the silver shawl she had packed. She always carried a shawl, as she tended to get a little cold. Once dressed, she began to style her hair and apply a little makeup.

She looked at herself in the mirror. Her dress fit just right, the silver shawl added a touch of elegance, and her hair and makeup were flawlessly done. She smiled, satisfied with her reflection.

Her attention was drawn to a photograph of Ryan's mom and sister on the wall. As she examined the pictures, her curiosity grew. She was eager to learn more about Ryan's background and family, hoping these glimpses into his personal life would reveal more about the man she was getting to know. She noticed another family picture of Mia and Ryan. They were younger and at an amusement park. The joy on their faces made her smile. She heard a gentle knock on the door.

"Emma, are you ready?" Ryan's voice called from the other side.

"Yes, I will be right out." She took one last look in the mirror, smoothing her dress and adjusting her shawl, and grabbed her purse. When she opened the door to leave, she felt a flutter of anticipation mixed with a touch of nervousness. The whirlwind of the past few days had brought unexpected experiences. With a deep breath, she stepped out, eager to see how the day would unfold and ready to face whatever surprises lay ahead.

C H A P T E R 22

W E D D I N G P A R T Y

At the church, Theo opened the door to the sedan, his hand shaking as he helped Mia out of the car. He let out a low "wow" once he saw her in her wedding gown, radiant from the inside out. He had the honor of walking her down the aisle. "It's time," he said, grasping Mia's hand and leading her into the church, where they waited for the music to start, and the procession to begin.

As Ryan walked by, leading first Jacob's mother, then Anne to their designated seats, Emma thought he looked like a Spanish James Bond in his tuxedo. Heading toward the front of the church, his piercing gaze met hers, and his face lit up with joy. Emma felt herself blush.

Then came the bridal procession, and at last, the bride and Theo, who gave her hand to Jacob. Mia and Jacob stood at the altar, lost in each other's eyes.

"I can't believe we are actually doing this," Mia whispered.

"I know! It feels amazing," Jacob replied, squeezing her hand.

They turned to face Father Alito, the priest officiating the ceremony. As he began, they exchanged glances, smiling at each other.

Soon they had exchanged vows and rings, their eyes never left each other's, and Father Alito proclaimed them husband and wife before the church. "You may now kiss the bride."

Mia and Jacob passionately kissed before turning to their family and friends waiting on either side of the aisle.

"I now officially present Mr. and Mrs. Jacob Roman."

They beamed at each other in pure bliss and walked down the aisle, followed by the rest of the wedding party.

As photographers snapped pictures, Emma couldn't help but notice the way Tina, Mia's maid of honor, moved to stand by Ryan every chance she could, to take his arm as she talked with him. Was it familiarity or something more? A knot tightened in her stomach, her mind racing through the possibilities. Did they share a history of which she wasn't aware?

The wedding group walked over to the gazebo for the official photographs. Mia stood out as a vision of timeless elegance. A delicate tiara sat atop her head, reminiscent of the one Meghan Markle wore at her royal wedding, adding a regal touch to her sleek look. Her white satin mermaid dress, simple yet stunning, hugged her hourglass figure perfectly, radiating grace with every step.

Ryan approached her, his eyes softening. "Mia, you remind me so much of Mom," he said, his voice carrying a mix of pride and emotion. "She'd be so proud of you today."

Mia smiled, her eyes glistening slightly, as she hugged him back. "Thank you. That means everything."

Ryan scanned the crowd, searching for Emma and spotted her standing to the side, watching the newlyweds pose for photos. He could not resist going over to her and taking her hand. "Hey, you," he said "What are you doing over here by yourself?"

Emma looked up at him, a smile spreading across her face. "Watching you all take your photos."

"I swear, if we take one more group picture, I'm going to start charging for photographs," he whispered, making her laugh.

Suddenly, the thought of not capturing this moment with her struck him. He wanted to remember this day, this feeling, and the person standing beside him.

He got Mia's attention. "Hey, would you mind if I took a photo with Emma?"

Mia grinned. "Go for it."

Ryan turned back to Emma, "Would you take a photo with me?" His gaze softened as their eyes met, something unspoken passing between them.

"Yes, of course," she said and felt her heart skip. There was a sincerity in his expression that caught her off guard, an invitation to be part of his world for just a little longer. And the photo? Was it a keepsake? They walked toward the photographer hand in hand. She wondered what this meant, if it meant anything at all.

After the photographer was done, Ryan thanked the photographer before turning to Emma. "Let's head to the reception."

Emma smiled and nodded, taking his arm as they approached the church. She had noticed Tina, the maid of honor, and Ken, the best man, conversing. It became apparent that there was nothing between Ryan and Tina. He seemed to only have eyes for her.

Almost as if to confirm he wanted her, not Tina, Ryan

turned to Emma, his expression serious. "You know what? I'd like to walk in with you, Emma."

Emma's heart skipped a beat. The gesture felt both bold and significant. It wasn't just a matter of tradition but a public statement.

"I'll walk in with you."

"Wait here. I'll be right back," he said and ran over to the church reception hall.

Emma waited, thinking about his choice to walk in with her, to show the two of them as a couple, and how it felt like a step toward something more meaningful.

The family reception at the church had its own DJ, and with the photos over, he flashed the lights to let the reception guests know it was time to announce the wedding party.

Ryan came back and joined her, giving her a wink as he took her hand again.

"Ladies and gentlemen, please give a warm welcome to the wedding party!"

Ryan felt overwhelmed with pride as they made their way to the front of the reception door, Emma's hand in his. He felt like he was on top of the world, surrounded by the family he loved most.

For Emma, it all seemed like a dream, something she had never experienced before. If someone had told her last week that she would have an accident, then a bout of forgetfulness, get lost, but meet the nicest, kindest guy, who also happened to be a doctor, and with whom she had an unusual but compelling connection, she would have thought they were joking. But she must admit, it felt good, especially holding his hand as she smiled at him.

"Please give a warm welcome to the bride's aunt and uncle,

Anne and Theodore Garcia, who are stepping in to honor Mia's late mother, Luna," the DJ announced. The crowd clapped and cheered as Theo and Anne made their way to the front of the reception hall, holding hands as Marc Anthony's *"Vivir Mi Vida"* played softly in the background.

It was lovely, the way the songs were chosen to honor each couple.

"And now, let's welcome the parents of the groom, Kathy and Lee Roman!" The guests applauded as Jacob's parents came thought the doors, their entrance accompanied by Frank Sinatra's "The Way You Look Tonight."

The DJ then turned to the microphone and said, "Please welcome the best man and the maid of honor! Let's hear it for Ken and Tina!" The crowd erupted in cheers as Ken and Tina entered together, dancing to DJ Khaled's "All I Do Is Win."

Finally, the DJ declared, "And now, please welcome the bride's brother, Ryan, who picked a special song for Emma!" The DJ changed the song to "My Girl" by The Temptations. Emma smiled shyly, feeling a flutter of excitement as Ryan put her hand through his arm and he led her through the reception hall as the guests clapped and a few whistled.

Emma Moment: *Ryan picked that song? It feels like he's trying to tell me something.*

The DJ turned off the lights, started rolling the drums, and then announced, "And now...the couple you've all been waiting for, please welcome the newlyweds, Mr. and Mrs. Roman, Mia and Jacob," as the couple entered the reception.

Every pair of eyes in the room turned to look at Mia and as

they made their way to the center of the floor, there was a loud cheer, and guests tapped their utensils against the glass.

Before long, the wedding reception was in full swing, and the DJ announced it was time for the bride and groom's first dance. KC and JoJo's "All My Life" came over the speakers as the couple took to the dance floor.

As the videographer finished filming the first dance, the music changed to "Mia" by Bad Bunny and Drake.

Ryan and Emma were standing to the side, watching his sister and brother-in-law dance. Ryan turned to Emma with a hopeful look in his eyes. "May I have this dance?" he asked, holding out his hand.

Emma's heart skipped a beat as she took his hand, and she didn't have to say anything. She just placed her hand in his.

The room was pulsing with the beat of the music. Ryan could not help but smile as he embraced Emma, pulling her warm body close against his.

As the music picked up, its fast and slow reggaeton beat was just what they needed. Emma swayed to the rhythm, her body moving perfectly with his.

Ryan could feel Emma's breath on his neck as they danced, sending shivers down his spine. For Emma, it was a romantic scene straight out of a movie, like *Dirty. Dancing,* a favorite of Emma's.

Emma and Ryan moved together, lost in the rhythm of the music, their bodies communicating everything they could not say with words.

As they moved around the dance floor, Ryan leaned in close to Emma's ear and whispered to Emma, "*Mia.*"

Mine.

She tripped, not expecting him to say that to her. "Sorry, Ryan."

"I got you. It's okay. I wanted you to know what I am thinking right now."

Emma's heart raced with anticipation, and she looked into his eyes, her face lit up with joy, and it felt like they were floating in the air. She did not want the song to end.

But it didn't end. They danced under the soft, twinkling lights as the evening wore on. Soon the room was filled with the gentle hum of conversation and the clinking of glasses, while the faint strains of a love song played in the background. They moved in sync, laughing and enjoying each other's company as they glided across the floor.

As they continued to dance, their conversation flowed effortlessly. Each revelation drew them closer, deepening their bond with each step. The warmth of their connection was evident as they discovered more about each other's dreams and passions.

They talked about everything, and Emma asked him what made him want to be a doctor.

"You know, I've always had a fascination with bones. When I was young and broke my arm, I was obsessed with learning everything about them. I'd constantly ask to go to the museum to see the dinosaur exhibits. *Jurassic Park* is still my favorite movie."

Emma laughed. "I've always loved to write and read. It's like creating little escapes for people and traveling the world through stories. And I'm a huge Disney fan. I'm obsessed with pastel pink, and Minnie Mouse is one of my favorites. Disney World has this magical charm that always makes me feel like a kid again."

"I can see why Disney World would be magical for you."

Emma laughed softly. "It really is. I guess we both have our own kinds of magic."

As "I'll Be There for You" by The Rembrandts filled the reception hall, Ryan turned to Emma. "I requested this for Mia. It's time for me to dance with my sister."

Emma nodded as Ryan scanned the room. The soft glow of string lights bathed the guests in a warm, golden light while the joyful buzz of conversation filled the air. Ryan's eyes found Mia, the stunning bride, gracefully dancing with her husband.

With a determined stride, Ryan made his way across the dance floor. He tapped Jacob on the shoulder to cut in, and as Mia looked at him, he grinned and said, "How you doin'?" with a Joey accent and a playful chuckle.

Mia burst out laughing, they had long been using that playful exchange from their favorite show, *Friends*.

"She's all yours, "Jacob said, handing Mia to Ryan before he stepped away.

The upbeat song seemed to amplify their shared laughter and the special bond they had. Brother and sister.

After a few minutes, Mia leaned in with a grin, teasing, "Took you way too long to dance with me, but just so you know, that Joey line was totally worth the wait."

Ryan laughed and twirled in a circle, making her throw her head back and laugh with him.

Ryan glanced over at Emma, who was sitting at a nearby table, talking with Jacob's parents.

"I see you're getting along well with Emma," Mia remarked, catching his gaze.

Ryan grinned. "Yeah, she's great," he said, looking back at Emma.

Mia tilting her head to the side, a playful grin on her face. "You two seemed pretty cozy earlier."

"I can't help it, Mia. Emma's special. She's easy to talk to. We both want to help others. It's refreshing to meet someone who shares that passion."

"Well, that's great. I'm happy for you."

As the reception began to wind down, a small group of elders said their goodbyes and left the reception, and they closed down the church hall, with the rest of the guests heading for Theo's home and the after-party.

CHAPTER 23

A MOMENT WITH HOPE

Emma Moment: *I want you to know that you are never alone. Evil influences cannot touch you when you raise your vibrations by meditating. Raising your vibration surrounds you with divine light, keeping you safe from any darkness or negativity that may come your way. I've seen how darkness can envelop someone, especially when they're grappling with deep grief or hurt. It's like a heavy shroud that clouds their energy, making them vulnerable to negative forces. This darkness can seem almost tangible, an oppressive weight that dampens their spirit and saps their strength. But when you raise your vibrations, you're creating a protective barrier around yourself. This divine light acts as a shield, preventing negativity from taking hold and offering you clarity and strength. It helps you see through the shadows and navigate your path with renewed resilience.*
You become a beacon of light.

The house was full of laughter, clinking glasses, and bass that wanted to live inside Emma's skull. Theo and Anne greeted guests at the door. Ryan guided the rest toward the backyard, where the party was already in full swing.

Emma leaned close to him. "I need a minute to reset. It's loud."

Ryan gave a quick nod of understanding and let her slip down the hall.

She found her bag in Ryan's room, shook two small pills into her palm, and carried them down the hall. In the kitchen, she grabbed a water bottle from the counter, twisted it open, and swallowed the pills. For a moment, she lingered there, palms pressed against the cool surface, waiting for the dull ache in her head to ease, but the music from outside still pounded like someone playing the drums right next to her ear.

Emma walked back through the living room, where Alyssa sat tucked close to two older cousins, giggling at something on a phone screen. Emma leaned down.

"I'm going to step outside to make a call. It's too loud in here."

Alyssa gave a quick nod and turned back to the conversation, already absorbed again.

The quiet was a relief after the loud music inside. Emma followed her intuition, turning left. A sudden sharp ache tugged at her chest, catching her off guard. She slowed, blinking against the sting in her eyes, and kept walking past the second house.

As the air shifted, Emma felt it because she was an empath. A thread of sadness, what felt like heartache, lingered around her.

By the third house, Emma saw her. A porch light glowed amber, revealing a teenage girl curled into an oversized rocking chair. Her pajama bottoms were splashed with happy yellow emoji faces, a jarring contrast to her blotchy eyes. The chair creaked in a slow rhythm as she rocked back and forth, her gaze darting between the empty space beside her and back toward Emma.

Emma lingered at the foot of the steps, giving her space.

"Hey," Emma said gently. "I'm Emma."

The girl brushed her hair back from her face, watching Emma warily. The rocking slowed.

"I'm Hope."

Emma lowered herself onto the bottom step. "Mind if I sit? My head's killing me. The music next door is fun until it isn't."

Hope gave a shrug, somewhere between careless and defensive, but it was permission enough.

Silence stretched between them, filled only by a few flies circling the porch light and the faint bark of a dog down the block.

"Rough night?" Emma asked.

Hope rubbed her sleeve under one eye as she shifted slightly in the chair. "Yeah."

Her shoulders sagged as she pulled her legs up, wrapping her arms around her knees. Her eyes drifted toward the front yard, vacant and far away. "I'm trying to decide what to do."

Emma tilted her head, keeping her tone light. "Well, you don't have to decide alone. Want to let me in on what it is?"

Hope picked at the hem of her pajama pants, twisting it into a rope. The sad emoji expression on her face as she took a deep breath, and then, finally, she let out a breath and said, "I saw my dad cheating with another woman."

Finally speaking the word out loud, she sighed as the rocking chair stilled. Emma stayed quiet, letting the truth breathe.

"At church," Hope added, her voice tinged with sadness. "In his office. He was with a woman with black hair. They were close, reading papers. He told her he's only ever loved one woman. He looked at her with love. She told him he needs to move on, putting a hand on his shoulder. As if telling him she was there for him with this look of love on her face," a single tear she brushed away with her other sleeve.

"He's always told my mom she's the only one." She dropped her gaze. "I was in the doorway. He didn't see me. I stepped back. Closed the door. I was in shock and couldn't breathe."

Emma's head pulsed, but not from the party. Emotion surged, tugging her into vision.

The porch dissolved.

A tidy office appeared, a cross on the wall, and a window spilling light across the desk. A man with dark hair held a page. Across from him stood a woman with sleek black hair, holding a sheet in her hand.

"I have loved one woman all my life," the man said.

"You keep telling me that," the woman replied. "But you have to move on." The woman laid one hand on his shoulder.

In the doorway stood Hope, eyes wide with hurt. She backed away, closing the door behind her.

Inside, the black-haired woman laughed, spun once, hugging the page. Emma glimpsed the title, Safe Haven Movie Script.

The vision vanished. The porch light and flies returned.

Emma exhaled. "This may sound a bit crazy to you, but I'm a psychic medium. I had a vision, and your dad was rehearsing lines from a script. That woman was not into your dad. She was acting. Rehearsing a scene. That sheet of paper was a script. It wasn't what you thought."

For a moment, she sat still, at a loss for words. "It wasn't?"

Emma kept her tone steady. "No, it wasn't."

Hope dragged a hand through her hair and sat up straight in the chair. "The way he said it. It sounded real, like he meant every word. Like he was telling her the truth."

Emma shook her head gently. "It was from the script she was holding. He was helping her practice. The weight you heard in his voice came from the part he was reading, not from him."

Hope's eyes flicked up, searching Emma's face, still uncertain.

Emma's expression softened. "You know, it's kind of like when I quote Sophia from The Golden Girls. 'Picture it...' I toss out a quote of hers whenever I need a distraction. It doesn't matter if it exactly fits. It makes me laugh."

Hope blinked, caught off guard. "Does it work?"

"It breaks the moment."

The corner of Hope's mouth tugged upward despite herself. A small, genuine smile broke through before she pulled her expression back under control.

Emma leaned forward, resting her elbows on her knees. "Here's the thing. You saw something, thought the worst, and kept it to yourself to protect your mom. But holding it in hasn't helped. It's only worn you down."

Hope's chin dipped, her voice quiet. "I thought it would fade. It didn't. It got worse."

"Then you've got to tell her. And your dad. Just be honest. Say what you saw and how it made you feel."

Hope stood, arms folded tight across her chest. She took a few steps, then turned back toward Emma, her eyes sharp with uncertainty.

Emma rose from the step, closing the space between them

just enough. She met Hope's gaze squarely. "Nothing in life is simple. But talking it out helps take the sting out of the heartache and the worry."

The two stood facing each other, the porch light casting a soft glow across their features. For the first time, the silence between them felt different, as if the energy had shifted, lighter than before.

After a pause, Hope lowered herself onto the step, choosing one corner of the stoop. Emma sat at the other end, giving her space. Hope tilted her head back, studying the sky before glancing at Emma again.

"When you walked up," she said at last, "I saw someone with you. A woman in white, surrounded by light. Then she was gone. Who was that?"

Emma was surprised. "Ahh, you have the gift of sight. That was Angel. She let you see that you are not alone."

Hope nodded slowly, waiting.

Emma's voice softened. "When I tell people I am a psychic medium, they usually have a million questions. But you did not. That tells me you already know more than you let on."

Hope's laugh was small but real, breaking through the wall she had been holding. "You could see that, too?"

"Yes," Emma said warmly. "And you can, too. All you need is practice." She tilted her head, curiosity slipping through. "But Einstein?" Her voice trailed off.

Hope's eyes lit with a hint of pride. "I ask him for help with my science. I know it sounds weird."

Emma smiled, shaking her head. "Not weird. Smart. The spirits help us when we ask them. You asked Einstein for help, stick with him and his crazy hair."

Hope laughed, tipping her head back just enough for a curl

to fall across her face. She brushed it behind her ear, the sound lighter than it had been before. "I ask for school stuff, information, especially in science. I want to be a doctor."

Emma nodded thoughtfully, still marveling at her. "That makes sense." She could not help but admire the idea of a teenager seeking advice from a genius of the past.

Emma glanced at the clock on her phone and realized it was getting late. She stood and looked at Hope. "Can I hug you?"

"Yes," Hope replied, her voice soft.

The embrace was quick but grounding, a spark of comfort passing between them.

When they pulled apart, Hope's demeanor had shifted. She seemed lighter, more hopeful, a stark contrast to the heaviness she had felt before.

Emma reached into her purse and handed Hope a sage kit and a selenite crystal. "Here. I want you to have this. You can use both to cleanse yourself. Try meditating. It will keep you grounded and help you feel calmer."

Hope's eyes widened. "Oh wow. Thank you, Emma."

Emma's fingers fluttered over Hope's phone, quickly typing in her number before handing it back to her. "Let's stay in touch," she said with a small smile, hoping to convey her willingness to be there for Hope if needed. "You can always reach out to me," she added, making eye contact and emphasizing the words softly.

"Oh my God, Emma, thank you so much. I will go in and talk to my mom now."

"Please let me know how it goes."

"I will," Hope said as she hugged her again.

Wow, Emma thought, what a whirlwind of a night this has been.

CHAPTER 24

AFTER PARTY

Theo had transformed the backyard into an outdoor dance floor, and the party was in full swing.

Ryan moved about the yard with the infectious energy that had made him such a hit at countless parties before this one. His smile never wavered. He pushed through the crowd, checking on guests, ensuring everyone was having fun, and offering them something to drink.

Emma had only been in the yard a few minutes when Ryan watched her approach the DJ, standing close to him, and saying something into his ear. He could not hear what she said, but he saw they were getting quite cozy.

Ryan felt a pang of jealousy, and he tried to shake off the feeling, knowing how irrational he was being. The DJ could be Emma's father.

The DJ took the microphone. "Hello, everyone. I'm DJ Jack, and we have our first request of the night. So, get out on the dance floor for the Spice Girls' Wannabe!"

Ryan saw Emma take a few steps toward him, but Alyssa swooped in and swept Emma away, laughing as they held hands and danced. From where Ryan was standing, he watched her hips rocking to the beat and spinning gracefully with his cousin, and he smiled. Alyssa had kicked off those little birthday heels she was so proud of and was having the time of her life. And she saved him. He never liked the Spice Girls, so watching Alyssa dance with Emma was somewhat of a relief. When the song ended, Alyssa's mother raised a hand, signaling her from the table. Alyssa released Emma's hands and crossed the patio to her side.

Ryan had always had a soft spot for love songs. They made him feel good because he used to dance to them with his mom. The DJ switched up the tracks, and Sin Banderas's *Entra En Mi Vida*" played.

Without hesitation, Ryan stepped onto the dance floor, his movements confident and fluid. He took Emma's hand and twirled her around gracefully, making her smile with delight. Mia and Jacob joined them, and soon others joined in the dancing. Ryan pulled Emma close, so close she could feel his breath on her neck. His arms around her waist felt like home.

As they danced together, Ryan could not help but wonder where she had been all his life. He could not believe how lucky he was to have bumped into her at Penn Station. He knew that he wanted to keep seeing her.

After the song had ended, they stood near the speakers, his arm casually draped over her shoulder as the music pulsed behind them. His eyes drifted upward, past the glow of fairy lights strung in the trees, to the sparkling stars above. He pointed toward a faint cluster over the oak.

"The stars are putting on their own show tonight. A view like this is magical... and even more so with the person you are with." His eyes sparkled as they dropped from the sky to her face, starlight catching in his expression.

She turned, lips curving with a small smile. "It is indeed magical. Funny, you bring up magic. My grandmother Ariana used to tell my sister and me stories under skies like this. She told us a Native American folklore love story she learned from a shaman she studied with years before."

His grin softened, and he leaned in slightly, gaze steady, shoulder brushing hers. He did not press with questions, but the way he lingered, head tipped to listen, was answer enough. "A love story under the stars? Seems like the perfect night for it."

Her eyes lifted to the crescent moon, pale and thin above the trees. "It is the story of Naya and Atilar. Naya was a mortal girl, who did chores every morning around her family's farm. She milked the cows, fed the horses, and gathered eggs from the chicken coop. She was beautiful, with long, wavy black hair that spilled past her shoulders and eyes the color of honey that glowed even in the dim light of dawn. Atilar was no ordinary man. He was the god of the heavens, the keeper of the stars and space itself. His black hair fell past his shoulders, and he possessed unmatched strength. With one hand, he could lift a great stone and move it as if it were a fly. He had seen everything the skies could hold, but when he looked down and saw Naya, something stirred in him. A feeling he had never felt before.

He came down to earth in the hush of a new moon. Naya lifted her head, startled, but instead of fear she felt wonder."

Ryan's arm tightened slightly against her shoulder, a faint breath escaping as though caught in the image.

He leaned closer, a half-smile tugging at his lips. "Sounds like anyone who walked past her would stop and look."

"Indeed. They met again the next night, but he had to go, and they parted, promising to see each other soon," her voice carried on. "From then on, Atilar would come down with each new moon, which only lasted two days. They walked by the river, talking and laughing. Dreaming of being together. But gods are not free."

Ryan exhaled slowly, the crease between his brows deepening as if he were trying to picture it. "I could not imagine wanting to be with someone but only getting two days each month."

Emma's gaze lifted toward the sky, lingering on the moon and stars, then she turned back to him and said, "I couldn't either. However, I believe when love is present, you will do whatever it takes to be with the one you love."

"Let's sit here by the tree." He pulled a chair out for Emma, and he took the seat next to her. "Please tell me they did something to be together."

"Well, Atilar's family discovered what was going on and they grew angry. To them, mortals were not worthy of Atilar, because they were not gods. They told him love between them could not be. He must leave her behind."

Her words stopped for a moment. "But Atilar would not. He told them he would give up his powers, his immortality, all of it so he could be by her side."

"That is some kind of love," Ryan said, letting out a low whistle.

"You can imagine how the family reacted, since no god had ever dared such a thing. The family was filled with disbelief and anger. But Naya and Atilar would no longer hide. They stood before the court of the gods and asked to be allowed to marry."

Ryan's jaw set, eyes narrowing as if he were standing before that court himself.

"The gods pretended to agree. They smiled and promised union, but they were all jealous because they could see, how much Alitar and Naya loved each other, but wanted to keep them apart. The court made a decision that bound them together. Naya would become the Sun because of her eyes. Atilar the Moon because he made the heavens sparkle. They were cruel, making it so that each would see the other, yet never stand side by side. Day and night. Always close, always apart."

Ryan shook his head, letting out a deep breath he was holding in. A sigh escaped as he said, "How sad. To be in love and not be together."

Her lips curved as she turned her head slightly towards him. "It is, the shaman taught her that everything on earth, even plants, carries a spirit. Night and day. Alitar and Naya. My grandmother learned that sage was a powerful plant. When she practiced smudging, she said the smoke carried prayers and removed heavy energy, making space for the good energy. And she was right in more ways than one. The smoke could clear the stagnant air, and it's even been found that a room stays free of bacteria for a day after smudging."

Ryan tilted his head, his expression caught between doubt and curiosity. "You don't say?"

Emma gave a soft laugh. "She believed in these plants used by Native Americans for centuries. There are many plants that are used for healing and other purposes."

Ryan leaned back slowly, his half-smile hovering as though he was still deciding what to make of it.

She turned slightly toward him. "Love has allies where you least expect it. Atilar's mother, who loved her son, saw how deep his love was for Naya. When the vote was cast for their separation, she did not put her vote for what the other gods wanted. She made another wish instead. That only occurs during a new moon eclipse, when the Sun and Moon are together. Cloaked under the eclipse, both would get a moment long enough to hold each other, even if for a short time."

His eyes stayed fixed on hers as he moved his hand to hold her hand. A smile illuminated his face.

"And so, with his mother's vote, she had helped her son be with his beloved. During a new moon with an eclipse, Naya and Atilar can steal away to be together again. For those rare moments, they embrace. And from that embrace, the stars are born. Each light we see above us is a child of their love, a reminder that even the heavens cannot destroy what is true."

Ryan's hand caressed Emma's hand as she continued the story.

Her voice softened further. "But there is more. The shaman told my grandmother that Naya and Atilar made their own wish as well. They wished that if two souls meet under a new moon and fall in love during an eclipse, their bond will be infinite. The gods cannot undo that gift."

Her gaze lifted to the sky, where the moon shone brightly above the noise of the party. "That is why my grandmother believed eclipses carry a power beyond science. That everything on this earth is connected in love."

The wedding laughter and the rise of music in the distance felt far away.

His voice held a slow and thoughtful curiosity. "I saw the news, and two days ago there was a new moon and an eclipse."

A soft laugh escaped her lips, blossoming into a smile as her eyes met his. "As the Good Witch would say...You don't say?" A gleam of magic shone in her eyes, and with it came a spark of attraction that lit the air between them. They felt the energy tonight as it carried the vibes still being felt from the eclipse.

Their eyes held, and for a moment, it felt as if the world had shifted. The love story hung between them, as if Naya and Atilar were blessing them.

From the corner of his eye, Ryan noticed Theo leaning closer to Anne, whispering something quickly in her ear. She nodded, her gaze turned anxiously toward the house, and they both slipped away, disappearing into the shadows by the back entrance.

Emma nudged Ryan with a laugh, pulling his attention back to her. He was tempted to follow Theo and Anne for a moment, but seeing Emma's smile, he brushed it off. Perhaps they just needed a moment alone.

Then he saw Anne come back, talking casually with some of the guests as she moved through the crowd. So all was good, he thought.

He stepped back in the shadows with Emma, holding her close, their bodies pressed together in a tender embrace. As their faces drew nearer, he gazed into her eyes, his own filled with warmth and affection. With a gentle smile, he leaned in, his lips hovering just inches from hers, creating a moment of shared breath and anticipation.

"Alright, ladies! Mia will toss the bouquet now. So, all the single ladies, get on the dance floor!" Anne held the microphone as she now stood on stage.

Ryan's shoulders slumped as he let out an audible sigh and stepped away. He ran a frustrated hand through his hair, his eyes narrowing in irritation. Each interruption felt like a cruel twist of fate, as if he and Emma were night and day.

Emma shot Ryan a knowing glance. She rolled her eyes and bit her lip, her frustration evident in her tight grip on his hand. They had been so close to sharing a kiss, and now it seemed like their special moment would be snatched away again.

"Looks like fate has our number tonight," he whispered in her ear. "But I promise you, this isn't the last of us."

Her face lit up like a flame as she blushed.

Emma chose to sit out the toss and let the other single women attempt to catch the bouquet. The DJ paused the music twice while Mia faked her toss. Emma was looking down at her phone when she looked up, Mia smiled and threw the bouquet right at her.

Emma stared up in shock. She caught it, or was hit with it, and laughed, looking right at Mia.

"So, Emma," Anne said into the mic, "Looks like you are next. Now the garter!"

The garter's symbolic significance was not lost on him; it represented the next step in a journey he was eager to embrace.

Jacob removed the blue garter to whistles and laughter.

With Emma having caught the bouquet, the idea of commitment and marriage was now on his mind. He felt a sudden surge of determination, his heart racing with the thought of possibly sharing that future with Emma.

Mia and Jacob shared a knowing smile as they looked at Ryan.

"Ryan!" Jacob called out, and Ryan looked up in time to see the blue lace descending from the air before it landed in his hands. He looked up from the garter with a wide grin to thank Jacob, who gave him one final wink before returning his attention to his new wife.

Emma Moment: *The bouquet and the garter. Sometimes, these little moments can be more than a coincidence. They might just be pointing in a new direction.*

Emma was standing in the center of the dance floor when someone brought a chair for the garter ritual. She looked up and saw Ryan looking gorgeous and looking at her.

It was time for Ryan to finish the garter ritual. He walked toward the DJ, feeling determined.

"Play Marvin Gaye's Let's Get It On." He told him and handed him a small piece of paper. "When I give you the cue, switch it to the other song on the paper."

DJ Jack nodded.

Ryan sauntered over to Emma, perched in a white chair at the center of the room. Every sway of his hips elicited an eager gasp from her parted lips. She held her breath in anticipation as the buttons on his shirt burst open with each seductive movement, reminiscent of Magic Mike himself. The surrounding crowd roared excitedly and clapped in unison as Ryan slowly inched down to his knees, placing his hands on Emma's legs with fierce intensity in his gaze.

The DJ switched the song to LL Cool J's "Doin' It."

Emma was the center of attention, but she could only sit there as his touch ignited a fire within her. Ryan was kneeling in front of her, his shirt open, and she could see the sweat beading on his chest. He slowly slid the blue garter up her leg, causing Emma to feel her face flush and she bit her lip in anticipation. As the garter reached her thigh, she grabbed his hand, and the party crowd whistled and laughed, but before either of them could move, the night sky erupted in a dazzling fireworks show above them. Everyone turned their eyes toward the skies.

It was the week of the Fourth of July celebrations.

Ryan took Emma's hand and pulled her to her feet. With time frozen, they stood together, the spectacular display overhead, but they were feeling only the intense heat radiating between their bodies.

A bead of sweat slid down Emma's temple. She wiped it with the back of her hand, then looked up at Ryan with a sheepish smile. "It's getting warm out here."

Ryan tilted his head, eyes scanning her face. "You okay?"

"No. Yes," she said quickly, brushing a strand of hair behind her ear. "I just need a minute."

He grabbed her hand to stop her. There was something in his expression that softened. "You know, if you did not walk away right now, I might have done something really dumb."

"Like what?"

"Like kissing you."

She did not answer right away. She couldn't speak. She wanted that kiss. She was afraid if she spoke, she would tell him to kiss her. She placed her hand on his arm and said, "Just give me a moment. I will be back," she said, her voice barely above a whisper.

As she turned toward the house, she gathered her hair and twisted it up, securing it with a clip from her purse.

Ryan watched her go, letting out a breath he had not realized he was holding.

CHAPTER 25

EMMA'S GRACE & THE LAST DANCE

While Ryan waited for Emma, he decided to kill time by thanking DJ Jack for playing his song requests. He walked over to Jack. "Thanks, man."

"No problem, anything for Emma," DJ Jack said.

Ryan took a half-step back, his curiosity piqued. "What do you mean anything for Emma?"

"Ah, the surprise. Why I'm here. Looks like the cat is out of the bag now," Jack said, a smile playing at the corners of his lips.

Ryan's mind raced as he processed Jack's cryptic words. The hint of a secret or deeper connection involving Emma left him on edge, eager for more information.

"Last night, I got a call from Emma asking for speakers. I knew I had to do more for her. She has been my rock since my mother's death."

Ryan paused. The revelation that Emma had orchestrated the last-minute save made everything fall into place.

Then Jack continued, "Emma deserves nothing but the best, and this is the least I can do." He pressed a button on his computer, which cued the next playlist of songs, and he hit another button to activate the flashing colorful lights.

"What did Emma do for your mother?" Ryan asked. "I'm genuinely curious."

Jack's eyes softened with a blend of gratitude and nostalgia. "You know, Emma isn't just kind; she's something truly special. I still remember when she first came into my mom's life. My mom, Teresa, was a fiercely independent woman, set in her ways. But Emma won her over quickly. I remember the day I came home and found Emma sitting at my mom's kitchen table, chatting away. My mom had always been a bit skeptical of new faces, but not with Emma, who could light up my mother's spirit in a way I hadn't seen in years."

Ryan took in Jack's words, feeling the depth of the sentiment behind them.

Jack's eyes softened. "My mom was in the early stages of Alzheimer's, and sometimes she'd get disoriented. One day, she walked out and forgot how to get back in. Emma found her and helped her find her way home. She even set up a reminder system with a star on her front door so my mom would remember where to go."

He laughed softly, shaking his head. "Emma didn't stop there. When my mom's condition worsened, Emma was always around. She'd come by, read to her, and just be there. She became like the daughter I never had, loving my mom like her own *abuelita*. Emma even intervened when a home health attendant mistreated my mom once. She confronted the attendant, defended my mom, and even ended up in a bit of a scuffle to make sure she was safe. Emma's fierce loyalty and protectiveness are beyond anything I've seen."

Ryan listened, moved by Jack's story.

Jack added, "When my mom's memory faded, Emma stayed by her side. She even helped me understand that although my mom couldn't speak, she still communicated in her own way. Emma taught me how to recognize signs from my mom, which was a comfort. When my first child was born, I saw a white orb around his crib, and Emma told me it was my mom watching over the baby."

He smiled wistfully. "Emma has this incredible gift. Even now, when my son talks, just chatters to seemingly no one, he says Nana. I know it's my mom because Emma saw her spirit. Her gift has blessed my family in more ways than I can count."

Jack's eyes glimmered with emotion. "She is worth more than gold," he declared, his voice full of conviction. "I would do anything for her."

"You know, Ryan," Jack added. "That's part of why I'm here today. I genuinely believe whoever marries her will win the ultimate prize."

"That's quite a compliment. Emma must be truly special to you."

"She is. I've seen her bring so much joy and support to those around her, especially during their tough times. I want the best for her and am grateful for everything she's done."

A sudden flashback washed over Ryan. He was watching Emma emerge from the bathroom yesterday. Her face was glowing with the purest, most radiant smile he had ever seen, and he had wondered what had caused it. She had a vision. But now a secret understanding dawned on him, and he knew exactly why she was so filled with joy. She had known their DJ was going to cancel, and she had called Jack and fixed it.

Just then, both Jack and Ryan looked up as Emma walked toward them. Her hair was now pulled back into a loose bun, with strands of brown and subtle blonde highlights softly framing her face.

As she approached, Ryan could not help but admire the gentleness that seemed to be around her.

"Welcome back," he greeted her warmly.

Emma's smile widened. "I hope I wasn't gone too long."

"No, not at all," Ryan reassured her, before he saw Theo signaling for him to come over. "Excuse me for a minute. I'll be right back," he said to Emma and gave her a wink. "Save the last dance for me."

Emma felt her cheeks flush as she watched him walk away, and a flutter in her chest at the thought of dancing with him later.

Emma smiled at Jack. "I'm so glad you're here, Jack. Thank you so much. You saved what would have been a disaster tonight."

"You know I would do anything I can for you," Jack hesitated, glancing at the clock before he looked at Emma. "It's winding down now. Almost time for the last dance."

"You have been a good friend."

"You made such a difference in my mother's life."

Emma tilted her head, smiling softly. "Your mom was such a wonderful person."

"You brought her such joy. The way you'd surprise her with flowers or bring her a cake for no reason at all. She'd laugh and say, '*La niña Emma me trajo flores,*' or 'She got me a cake, and it's not even my birthday.' It meant the world to her."

He paused before he spoke again. "You have a gift, Emma, and it's something I can never repay."

They both were quiet for a moment, remembering Teresa.

"My mother always said, *'Qué niña más dulce y buena.* That you are a sweet, good girl." I agree.

Mia and Jacob had requested a salsa song by Marc Anthony for their last dance, which was coming up, and everyone joined in the fun. Even Alyssa was dancing with the crowd.

Ryan twirled Emma confidently, loving how her laughter blended with the rhythm of the music.

"You've got some impressive moves there," Emma said. "Did you take dance lessons?"

Ryan grinned, holding her close as they danced. "Actually, my mom taught me. She was a fantastic dancer. Salsa was her favorite."

"Well, it's clear she taught you well. You make it look effortless."

Ryan chuckled, enjoying the compliment. "Thanks. I'm glad I can share a dance with someone who appreciates it. Someone special."

Emma felt her heart hitch at his words. The music pulsed around them, and it felt like the world outside had faded away for a moment, leaving just the two of them.

The musical notes of a salsa song made the speakers vibrate as the speakers changed colors from red to green, blue, and back again to red. Mia and Jacob spun into the center of the patio, laughter tangled with rhythm, and the crowd surged after them. Chairs scraped back, heels tapped against the flagstone, and even the shy guests were pulled forward by the tide of music.

Ryan caught Emma's hand and pulled her into the floor of dancers, his grin daring her to resist.

"Not escaping," he said, spinning her beneath his arm.

"I do not know if I can keep up." She meant to sound teasing, but her breath betrayed her.

He twirled her into the sea of dancers, feeling the musical vibes in his bones.

The beat caught her feet before her mind could protest, her laugh bursting out as he spun her under his arm.

"You are keeping up just fine." His smile widened. "My mom loved to dance. Salsa was her passion."

"She must have been something."

"The best. Every Saturday was cleaning day, and she would be blasting Marc Anthony loud enough for the neighbors to complain. She always dragged me in, spinning me across the living room floor until I forgot the broom in my hand." He winked, pulling her into a spin that ended a step too close.

The image of Ryan, younger and holding a broom, dancing with his mother was sweet. It felt like his suit of armor was falling away.

The song ended, and Emma moved away, heat shimmering across her skin. She moved toward the edge of the patio, chest rising fast, telling herself she only needed air. Before she could catch her breath, Ryan appeared at her side with a cold bottle of water, as though he had read her mind.

She pressed it to her lips. "I did not realize it would get this hot out here."

There was a long pause.

Ryan's eyes glinted. "I heard about your secret. Calling Jack in to sub DJing like that. You saved the night."

Emma froze mid-sip, the water cooling her mouth while a flush rose along her neck. She had not done it to be noticed. She had done it for Mia. For her to have a beautiful wedding party and everything turned out the way it was supposed to.

"So much for keeping that quiet." She groaned and tipped her head back with a sigh.

"It surprised me to find out. Just so you know, Jack slipped and told me."

Her fingers tightened on the bottle. No one was supposed to know, because it was a gift from her heart.

"It was not a big deal," she brushed a strand of hair from her temple. "I just did not want Mia disappointed."

"That is the thing." His voice lowered, so no one could hear. "You did not do it for yourself. You did it for her. That says everything I need to know."

Heat from a slow shade of red was starting to form on her cheeks so Emma began to fan herself with her hands.

"You have a good heart and really care about people you do not even know."

"It's nothing."

"That is the point." His grin was quick, followed by a wink that left her pulse racing. He leaned in slightly, his shoulder brushing hers, his tone lighter again. "You are hard to figure out, Emma. One minute you are in the background trying not to be seen, and the next you are saving the night and pretending it was nothing. Keeps me on my toes."

Her lips curved, though she tried to hold it back.

"You sound like you enjoy that."

"I do."

His touch slid into hers again, slow but confident, as though the choice had already been made. "You saved the night, Emma. That makes this dance mine. Non-negotiable."

Her lips curved despite herself. "Bossy."

"Confident. There is a difference." His palm stayed warm against hers.

The following love song was slower, a melody that drew couples closer together. She let him guide her back into the crowd. His hand pressed steadily at her back, his lead effortless, and the noise around them dulled until all she felt was the closeness of him.

"You keep surprising me." His voice brushed her ear.

"I like that."

Her breath caught. Play it off, her instincts repeated. Laugh it away. But the look in Ryan's eyes made it impossible.

"Surprises are not always good," she managed.

"This one is." The certainty in his tone tugged at her chest harder than it should have.

She felt her body go from cold to hot.

The music rolled steadily, each beat pressing them closer. The sky was illuminated by the stars and the lights swaying in the light breeze. Ryan was watching her as if the rest of the world had vanished, as if the crowd was only background noise.

Her gaze broke away first, tracing the lights strung across the patio. Her heart beat out of rhythm, not with the music but with Ryan.

His hand on her back was an anchor. Without thinking, she leaned closer, her head resting against his chest. The sound of his heartbeat startled her, strong and even, beating to the same tone as her heart.

For a breath, she let herself stay there, letting his heartbeat guide her. A dangerous thought whispered that she could get used to this. She pulled away before she drowned in it, but Ryan's arm lingered at her waist. She did not step aside. Not yet.

The song ended, but they did not want to let go. The attraction between them was undeniable. Emma told herself it was nothing serious, but when she looked at Ryan's face, she knew deep down that it was something more.

Applause broke across the patio as Jack's voice boomed over the microphone. "Ladies and gentlemen, let's give it up for the newlyweds, Mia and Jacob!" Cheers and whistles rolled through the crowd, followed by his warm farewell. "May your love endure forever! And now, I bid you all goodnight. Get home safely, folks."

The noise dimmed as the party began to wind down. Guests drifted toward the exit, exchanging hugs and laughter, as the air cooled with the settling of the night. Emma stayed close to Ryan, his arm resting lightly on her back. For a moment, she let her head lean against his chest.

Her temples throbbed faintly, a reminder of the long day, but when Ryan glanced down at her, she only gave him a small smile. "I think the music caught up with me."

"You have done enough tonight," he said, voice low. "Go rest. I'll help Theo with the cleanup."

"You are sure?"

"I am." His touch brushed her arm, warm and grounding.

Emma hesitated, then nodded. "Thank you."

She turned toward the house with Alyssa and Alex, her steps slower now, and for the first time all night, she did not fight the pull of leaving someone behind. She felt his eyes on her until Mia's laugh carried across the patio.

Emma glanced back just in time to see Mia lean into her brother, her voice full of mischief. "You are so smitten with her. It is adorable. And now that she caught the bouquet and you the garter, maybe you will be next." She kissed his cheek and disappeared into the night with Jacob at her side.

CHAPTER 26

DIVINE REVELATIONS

Inside the house, Alyssa and Alex were heading down the hall.

"Good night," Emma said softly.

"Night," Alyssa replied with a smile. "Hope you feel better."

Alex gave a small wave. "Sleep tight."

Emma walked into the kitchen and grabbed a bottle of water from the fridge. She pressed it to her forehead as she made her way to Ryan's bedroom, the cold plastic easing the dull throb in her head.

Once inside, she quietly closed the door and changed into her pajamas. The soft fabric was a relief, and the AC too, after all the busy events of the wedding.

She sat on the edge of the bed, opened the water, and took two aspirin from the small bottle in her purse. After a few sips, she placed the water on the nightstand.

Then she reached under her pajamas and slid off the blue garter. She held it for a moment, brushing her fingers over the lacy fabric. Without a word, she lifted the pillow and tucked it underneath.

Climbing into bed, she pulled the covers up to her chin. She was tired, and sleep came quickly, wrapped in exhaustion and a small smile as she let herself remember how the night had unfolded with Ryan.

Emma awoke the next morning with the lingering feeling that something would happen today.

But it wasn't until she had left the bathroom and gotten dressed that she heard excited voices coming from the living room.

In the living room, Anne and Ryan appeared in a rush, Anne was already wearing her coat. Standing behind her was little Matthew, whose face was very flushed with fever, and his eyes filled with tears. He kept telling Anne that his head hurt, and she placed a cool hand on his forehead, confirming that he was burning up.

Emma's gut twisted with unease as she realized something was very wrong. She emerged from the hallway, her gaze following Anne as she bent down to lift Matthew into her arms. He looked up at Emma and gave her a weak smile. A sense of clarity she hadn't felt before swept over her.

The mishaps of her memory loss, the broken phone, and the confusion about where she lived, all seemed to converge at this very point. She realized that these struggles were meant for a reason. It was as if the universe had conspired to bring her to this place, at this exact time, to offer support when it was most needed. This was the moment her journey had led to. She was here to help.

Emma knelt beside Matthew, offering him a reassuring smile. "It'll be all right," she said softly. The two shared a hopeful glance, a mutual understanding passing between them.

Matthew regarded Emma with a trusting look.. "Mom, I want her to carry me," he proclaimed.

Anne's face softened into a gentle smile. "This is Emma, a friend of Ryan's." She faced Emma. "Do you mind?"

"No. Of course not." Emma picked up Matthew gently, feeling a profound sense of purpose.

"We need to go now."

Emma saw the worry in Anne's and gave her a reassuring nod.

"Angel told me," Matthew said quietly to Emma.

Theo was standing in the doorway. "Who is Angel?"

Ryan and Anne stood beside him. Confusion flickered across everyone else's faces in the room, but Emma understood.

Her eyes never left Matthew's as she replied, "You know her and have seen her, haven't you?"

Matthew nodded solemnly. "Yes, Angel came to visit me. She told me you were coming to help me."

Anne looked worried. "It's his fever. It's so high."

Matthew continued, "Angel told me that Emma was going to come and help me." He looked at his father and mother. "She said you would not believe it, so she gave me this." He opened his left hand, where a white feather lay in his palm.

The room was filled with confusion as Theo's eyes locked onto the white feather in his son's tiny hand. Emma, understanding the feather's significance, watched as the others tried to grasp its meaning.

"Where did you get that feather?" Theo asked.

Matthew smiled. "Daddy, I told you Angel gave it to me."

Emma hugged Matthew tighter, being careful not to make

him feel uncomfortable. She knew what she had to do. As she held her hand just above his chest, she silently willed the illness away, focusing all her energy and faith into the task.

With each repetition of her prayer, Matthew's flushed face, his fever, began to fade, and his labored breathing started to even out. His small, furrowed brow relaxed, and the tension in his tiny body eased.

The transformation was subtle but unmistakable. Emma's eyes remained fixed on him, her heart pounding with hope. The others in the room watched in astonishment as Matthew's color returned to a healthier hue and his breathing steadied. A visible change was unfolding before them, leaving them in a state of wonder and disbelief.

Emma Moment: *I closed my eyes, feeling the warmth of Matthew's small frame against me. As I focused inward, a vision began to take shape in my mind. I saw a heavy, dark rock lodged deep within his chest, representing the illness that burdened him. Each word of my prayer seemed to interact with this vision, gradually shrinking, and the rock began to disappear.*
With every repetition of my prayer, I could see the rock getting smaller and lighter, its oppressive weight diminishing. I could almost feel the transformation happening, as though my words were physically breaking down the mass.
It became clear that I had been given a gift. I had the power to heal, to remove the illness that had afflicted Matthew. This revelation filled me with a profound sense of clarity and resolve. I wasn't just here by chance; I was meant to be here, using my gift to make a real difference.

Warm sunlight streamed through the window, casting a

golden glow. The light around them seemed to grow brighter, casting an ethereal sheen on the room. A scent of roses filled the air. The once-warm sunlight now appeared almost heavenly, bathing the scene in a divine glow.

Everyone in the room was silent, captivated by the extraordinary sight that had unfolded before them.

Ryan stood there, transfixed. Anne was overwhelmed with emotion, her voice caught in her throat as she watched the white light that had engulfed her son fade. Theo watched in stunned disbelief, his knees buckling as he sank to the floor, overcome with emotion. Tears streamed down his face, glistening in the bright light. With a sense of reverence, he began reciting "The Lord's Prayer," his words were a testament to the miracle that had unfolded before him.

What they had just witnessed was undeniably a divine miracle, a supernatural event beyond any ordinary explanation.

Emma put Matthew down. "He's healed."

Anne lifted Matthew into her arms. He did not look tired or flushed anymore. She heard Theo repeatedly saying, "Thank you, God." Holding her son up, Anne thanked God for healing him.

Ryan was rooted in place, split between confusion and shock. He had seen all the doctor's notes, the tests that led them to believe that Matthew might need a new heart, though more tests were recommended. His concern had run deep and unspoken, bound by the need to respect the family's confidentiality.

He had not told Emma about this. In fact, he hadn't talked about it to anyone because he felt like a failure. He was a doctor, but he was not able to do anything himself.

He looked around the room and noticed Emma, who appeared just as astonished as everyone else. It was clear now that there was something beyond mere chance at play. Emma's presence, her uncanny ability to know things, felt almost too coincidental to ignore.

Emma said, "Mathew, you will be well."

Mathew looked up at her and replied, "I know. Angel told me so."

She accepted why she was there, at that moment in time.

The confusing events of the past few days aligned in her mind her memory loss, and the strange pull to this place. Each turn of events had led her to this boy, this house, this moment.

Anne ran over to Emma and embraced her, tears streaming down her face. Through sobs, she choked out, "Thank you for saving my son."

"You are welcome," she whispered, her voice tinged with a new understanding. She returned the embrace, offering solace through her tender touch. "You have an extraordinary child."

Theo rose from his kneeling position, took her hands, and thanked her.

"Your unwavering faith created this miracle, Theo. I was only an instrument to bring it to fruition."

Ryan spoke then, "You should take him to his doctor."

"Yes," Emma agreed, but she knew what they would find.

"Maybe we should get Matthew to the hospital and let the doctor check him out and run tests." Theo walked toward the door.

Emma watched them leave, but her thoughts ran deeper. It wasn't just about the strange occurrences anymore; it was about destiny, about trusting the journey despite not always under-standing it. A sense of peace settled over her; this was where she was meant to be.

CHAPTER 27

THE KISS

It had been a morning of miracles, Ryan thought as he came back inside after walking Theo, Anne, and Matthew to their car. As he came through the door, his heart raced with anticipation.

Emma. She was standing in the middle of the room and turned toward him as he closed the door. He could feel a powerful energy emanating from her very being, a benevolent force that captivated all present.

Without hesitation, he pulled her into his arms, holding her tightly with a fierce strength that spoke volumes of his feelings for her. As their eyes locked in an unspoken connection, sparks flew, and a fiery passion ignited between them, enveloping them both in a rush of excitement, undeniable attraction, and an unexpected sense of familiarity. The world around them blurred, and for that moment, it felt as if they were the only two people in it.

Ryan's pulse pounded in his ears as he lost himself in Emma's sparkling light brown eyes. The irresistible force pulling them together was undeniable, and with a boldness he did not know he possessed, he cupped her face gently, his touch firm yet tender.

For a moment, he gazed at her, taking in the warmth and softness of her skin beneath his fingertips, before leaning in and pressing his lips to hers, his heart racing with the electric intensity of their connection.

The spark that had ignited between them quickly grew into an all-consuming flame that left them breathless. Despite the traffic of the bustling street outside, where the distant noise and movement felt muted, their lips moved in perfect unison, driven by a primal desire that consumed them both, setting off a symphony of emotions, desire, passion, and longing rippling through their bodies. Their mouths moved in a frenzied dance, each breath a desperate plea for more.

It was a kiss fueled by raw desire and aching need, revealing the depths of their untapped passion.

As they pulled away, Emma's chest heaved with want, and her voice trembled as she whispered, "Wow."

Ryan burned with intensity as he quietly replied, "Worth the wait."

In that moment, they both knew that their fates were irrevocably intertwined, bound by an unbreakable bond forged in that passionate kiss.

A noticeable energy crackled in the air, causing their hearts to race and their lungs to burn for oxygen. They gazed at one another, leaving them both hot with desire and the need for another kiss.

But the spell was broken when Emma's phone started to ring. She glanced at the caller ID and saw 'Mom' flashing on the screen.

Mom? How...? "It's my mom!"

"You had better answer it."

She quickly answered the call and walked toward Ryan's room for privacy.

"Mom!" Emma heard the tremble of relief and emotion in her voice. "You won't believe what has happened to me!"

Her words flowed freely as she recounted on her experience, her excitement bubbling over. Her mother listened intently.

"You need to come see me in person. We must talk about this, and I need to hug you."

Tears rose in Emma's eyes as she whispered, "I love you, Mom."

She promised to come the next day, asked her to relay her love to her father, and promised her mother that she'd be texting Liz right after hanging up to let her know she was coming home.

After she finished the call and the text to Liz, Emma felt a deep sense of relief and peace, knowing that her journey home was now clear. She could reunite with her family with a full heart. She glanced at her phone one last time before putting it away, and she was shocked to see the screen display her phone contacts, complete with their telephone numbers, emails, and addresses. It was as if her phone had magically recovered, and all the lost information had reappeared.

Synchronicity.

Emma couldn't help but smile, feeling a deep connection and the sense of clarity, she had gained. It was a subtle yet profound affirmation that her journey, with all its twists and turns, had brought her to exactly where she needed to be.

Emma slowly zipped up her hoodie, feeling a sense of finality as she prepared to go home. With the fog of panic finally lifting, memories of her parents' house came flooding back. She reflected on the journey she had been through and the lessons she had learned along the way.

It was her angel, a guiding presence, who had told her she needed to learn three important lessons. First, she had learned compassion through her trials. Then, patience had come to her in moments of struggle. Finally, love had blossomed as the underlying force that connected her to others and herself.

As she thought about these lessons, Emma felt immense gratitude and a pure sense of understanding. Each lesson shaped her journey and brought her to this moment of clarity and homecoming.

Emma Moment: *Reflecting on my journey, I see how these lessons were woven into every experience I faced. My earlier fears and doubts about my gifts were part of my growth. I had to learn to face these fears to heal. By doing so, I've learned that embracing love and staying open to it is vital. My abilities are a part of my purpose, guiding me to help others and grow myself.*

As Emma gathered her things, her mind briefly wandered back to Ryan. Standing as she was on the threshold of her departure, she felt a surge of anticipation and longing.

The kiss they shared had been intense and meaningful, leaving her with a swirl of emotions she hadn't fully processed. The affection she felt was overwhelming, not just a fleeting desire, but something real.

Then, while packing her clothes, a vision formed. She paused as the image of Matthew took form. He was no longer a child, but a man of forty, standing on a podium, facing a judge in a black robe, one hand on the family Bible his beautiful wife held.

"I do solemnly swear that I will faithfully execute the Office of the President of the United States, and will, to the best of my ability, preserve, protect, and defend the Constitution of the United States."

And the crowd cheered as the vision slowly faded.

Her healing of Matthew was part of a greater plan. She envisioned him growing into a leader who would unite people not just across the United States but globally. The thought of his future, a time of great unity, brought her immense joy and reassurance, knowing that her actions today contributed to a world where harmony and progress could flourish.

She zipped her backpack closed, lastly tucking the blue garter in a pocket, and then she lingered, taking in Ryan's bedroom. They had just experienced something unique together, something she had never felt before, something that was just the beginning. She took one last look around the room and left.

Ryan met Emma in the living room, and he motioned for her to follow him. Together, they walked out toward the backyard. His expression was intense and unreadable as he turned to face her. "I have so many things I want to say, but I can't seem to find the right words. What you did was incredible. Have you ever done anything like that before?"

Her eyes never wavered from his. "No. I have never healed before. That was my first time."

He leaned closer, his gaze intense. "There's so much more I want to learn about you." He gently traced her lips with his finger, not to stop her from speaking but to savor the moment and their connection. Then he looked into her eyes again. "I want to understand more about what we all experienced earlier...about us. Together." He paused. "Would you have dinner with me?"

"On a date?" Emma asked, a faint smile tugging at the corner of her mouth.

"Yes, a date."

"I'd love to go on a date with you."

"Tomorrow," he said. "I don't want to wait for a Friday or Saturday night."

"Me, either."

She was not unhappy to be going home, and while she would miss this place and Ryan's family, she could not help but feel excited.

Ryan pulled her into his arms for one lingering kiss good-bye. He took her address and number, then ordered a taxi for her. With a playful grin, he said, "I guess it's a good thing you finally remembered your address."

The taxi pulled up. He opened the car door, and Emma slid in. She waved goodbye as the cab drove away, then she turned to look back, watching Ryan standing on the curb till the cab made a turn and she couldn't see him anymore.

Emma stared out the taxi window, thinking of Ryan, when a vision appeared before her. Through the glass, she saw Luna standing in the living room Emma had just left, smiling from ear to ear.

"Welcome to the family," she said with a wink.

Emma blinked, and the moment was gone. She laughed to herself, feeling content with Luna's approval. She now understood what Luna had meant when she had opened that door that first day and said, "We have been expecting you."

Her phone's incessant beeping alerted her to a new message. It was from Hope, and her heart quickened as she read it.

Hope: TY. I spoke to my parents like you said to, and it turns out Dad didn't cheat. He was helping someone run lines for a role. My mom knew all along. Guess I should've come forward sooner. P.S. My mom wants a kit too, and she wants to meet you. TTYL, Hope.

After she arrived back in Queens, Emma stepped out of the taxi, her hand tightly gripping her keys. She pushed open the glass lobby door and rode up to the third floor in the cramped elevator. As soon as she inserted her key into the lock of her apartment, she heard her sister's dog Mickey's loud bark through the door. With a smile, she opened the door and was immediately greeted by his enthusiastic jumps and slobbery kisses. His tail wagged wildly as he circled her, happy to see her home again.

"Hi, Mickey. Did you miss me?" she asked, reveling in the reunion.

Liz emerged from the bathroom, exclaiming, "Oh, look who's here!"

As Emma and Liz hugged, they exchanged a quick appraisal, their laughter filling the air. Emma dropped her duffle bag onto the floor beside the sofa and sank onto the cushions. "You will not believe everything that's happened to me this week." She sighed. "Honestly, it felt like something out of a soap opera."

"I couldn't remember my address, your phone number, or even what happened with Gary. He scribbled something down on a piece of paper, and poof! It vanished like magic. It wasn't just forgetfulness. It felt like my memory had been completely wiped out, like I was caught in some dramatic amnesia story-line. The concussion made it worse, I guess."

Liz, listening intently, got up and walked over to her wallet. She pulled out Emma's driver's license and handed it to her. "Gary gave me this," she said with a smile.

Emma took the license with a grateful nod. "Thank you."

As Emma stood up, thinking she would make her famous pink margarita cocktail, she asked Liz if she wanted one. Liz declined. Emma mixed the drink and took a long sip before settling back onto the sofa.

Liz sat down next to her, very close, and said, "And I hear you met someone."

"Gary spilled the beans, didn't he?"

"Yes. I even dreamed about him last night, but I'm guessing you already know what my dream was about."

The two sisters shared a hearty laugh.

Emma showed Liz the wedding bouquet of mixed roses, and she described Ryan's Magic-Mike-inspired dance while putting the garter on her at the wedding.

Liz could not stop oohing and aahing as she indulged in pizza. It was like no time had passed between them, and Liz was overjoyed to hear about Emma's exciting new relationship.

"Oh, and Ryan is a doctor. An orthopedist," Emma said.

"Get out of here. A doctor? You will quiet *todas las chimosas,* the family gossips who keep asking you if you have a boyfriend. I want to be there when you shut them down," Liz said with a laugh.

There was a loud knock at the door, and Mickey began to bark.

Emma and Liz exchanged a knowing look.

The building's intercom system was down.

"I'll check, just in case we are wrong." Liz went to the peephole, peering out into the hallway. She saw a man standing outside the door, a pretty good-looking man.

Emma pushed her aside, then she laughed and opened the door.

Ryan stood there, his smile familiar and welcome, as he explained he was unable to contain his eagerness until Monday night.

Both Emma and Liz stared back at him.

In unison, they said, "We were expecting you!"

Epilogue

It was July 4th again, exactly one year later, and Emma and Ryan walked toward Blend on the Water, a Latin American restaurant in Long Island City.

"It's so humid out here," Ryan commented, wiping sweat from his brow as they made their way through the holiday crowd, the sounds of fireworks already echoing in the distance.

"I know. The air is so thick." Emma sighed,

"We'll be able to cool off soon enough, once we get inside the restaurant," Ryan said cheerfully, placing his hand on the small of her back as he guided her to the door. His touch always made her heart race.

The restaurant was bustling with people, but Emma and Ryan made their way to the line. Emma could not help but look up at the beautiful floral ceiling, her eyes tracing the flowers and vibrant colors.

"I've never seen anything like this. It's beautiful."

Ryan smiled. "I knew you would love it."

As they waited, Ryan kept a watchful eye on his surroundings, making sure everything was going according to plan. This was the big day, and despite all her unique gifts, which too often still surprised him, he needed to surprise her. With the help of Mary and Liz, who had been instrumental in planning the surprise, everything was set for a memorable moment.

At reception, they were told there was a twenty-minute wait for their table. But Emma did not mind as she gazed out the window at the stunning views of Manhattan. The waterfront sparkled under the warm sun.

"Look how beautiful it is!" Emma exclaimed.

Ryan chuckled and took her hand. "Yes, it is. Come. I have something even more beautiful to show you."

Emma followed Ryan out of the restaurant and toward the waterfront.

Ryan stopped. "Okay, close your eyes."

Emma rolled her eyes but obliged, closing her eyes then letting Ryan lead her a few feet more, until he stopped her and said, "Okay. Now you can open them."

Emma opened her eyes, taking in the panoramic scenes spread out before her. Boats dotted the water with a stunning view of Manhattan in the distance. Behind them was the famous Pepsi-Cola Sign.

"It's lovely," Emma said.

He took her hand. "Come, let's walk." As they walked along the waterfront, Ryan pointed out different landmarks and shared personal stories about each one. Emma listened intently, her heart filled with joy at experiencing this beautiful place with someone she loved.

He gestured to the water and asked Emma if she could see someone on a jet ski. She turned her head, squinting against the sun's glare, but shook her head.

"Emma, I love you more than anything in this world." Ryan

took a deep breath, his heart racing as he got down on one knee. "Will you do me the honor of being my wife?" He held out a gleaming one-carat princess-cut engagement ring.

She gasped, overwhelmed, surprised, tears sparkling in her eyes, as she nodded eagerly. "Yes! Yes, Yes!"

He slipped the ring onto her finger and pulled her into a tight embrace and kiss.

Overhead were the warm sun and the playful antics of seagulls, and a large ship slowly cruised by, its horn blaring. The sudden noise diverted her attention momentarily. The blaring horn was followed by cheers and clapping.

From behind nearby structures, family members hiding and eagerly watching the couple's reaction popped out like jack-in-the-boxes. Their congratulations and applause filled the air. The surprise was a beautiful display of love and support, a moment of pure joy that they would cherish forever.

Emma's mind was reeling as she saw both families standing together, united. She had no idea that Ryan and her family had been scheming behind her back.

Mary moved toward Ryan, enveloping him in a tight embrace. "Welcome to the family," she said exuberantly.

Emma's dad, Mateo, followed suit, giving Ryan a firm pat on the back. *"Bienvenido, mi hijo, a la familia,"* he declared proudly.

Theo then turned his attention to Emma, engulfing her in one of his trademark bear hugs. "I'm so happy we can finally call you *familia,*" he said with a warm smile. Next, Anne also hugged her and said, "Welcome to the family."

Liz bounded over to Emma and threw her arms around her sister and best friend. "You have to let me be your maid of honor!" she exclaimed eagerly.

Alyssa was not far behind, tugging at Liz's sleeve. "And I will be the junior bridesmaid," she chimed in excitedly.

Matthew joined in, too. "And I'll be the ring boy!" he declared heartily with enthusiasm, his color good and showing no signs of illness that had divinely disappeared.

As they all laughed and hugged each other tightly, Emma felt a deep sense of belonging wash over her. She had yearned for a companion, a love who valued her for who she was, not just for her gifts. Her past fears of being sought after only for her abilities had often overshadowed her dreams of finding a true connection. But then, the past year, everything had changed. She had found Ryan.

As they gathered around for a moment of bonding and love, Emma caught a glimpse of Luna's reflection, shining in the front door window of the restaurant. She managed to throw Luna a quick, knowing smile at that moment. However, when she turned back after hugging Matthew, Luna was gone.

Emma could feel the warmth, knowing that Ryan's mom approved of their union, even in spirit. It felt like a perfect moment frozen in time, one filled with love and acceptance. Emma took a deep breath, savoring the feeling of being surrounded by loved ones and the knowledge that Luna's blessing would always be with them.

Ryan's friends Harry, Mike, and Justin approached, their smiles wide and genuine.

"Congratulations, you two!" they said, giving Ryan a hearty pat on the back. "Here's to a lifetime of happiness! May your days be filled with love and laughter."

Justin shook Ryan's hand and turned to Emma. "I'm so happy for you both."

A few moments later, Nurse Andrews said, "Emma, I'm thrilled for you. The ring is stunning."

Leaning in close, she whispered with a playful grin, "You know, I won the office pool on who would win Ryan's heart!"

Emma laughed. "I guess I'm the real winner!

After many well-wishes and a round of catching up, they finally arrived back at the restaurant, where Ryan had reserved a small celebration party. All the family members were there to celebrate the happy news.

Amidst the party, there were Jacob and Mia, who was pregnant and due any day now. As she embraced Emma warmly, her face lit up. "I'm so happy to share this moment with you."

About four months earlier, Theo mentioned doing a DNA test and expressed his curiosity about his family heritage. He had recently received the results, which revealed a surprising discovery. Theo had a sister he didn't know about.

Today was Emma's first meeting with Carmen and her son, Micah. Theo and Anne introduced them. Not only had Theo, along with Anne, welcomed Carmen into their lives, but he had also taken on a mentoring role for Micah. Their bond had grown strong.

"Hi," Emma said as she extended her hand to Carmen.

"Theo and Anne have told me so much about you, Emma," Carmen said, "and this is my son, Micah."

Micah extended his hand, too, but when he shook hands with Emma, they both felt the electric shock and let go immediately. He looked up at the same time as Emma. They both laughed.

Before long, Ryan joined Emma and slipped his arm around her as they watched their families, the warmth and happiness in the room settling over them. It was then that Emma caught a glimpse of Angel standing nearby.

Ryan leaned over to whisper in her ear, "I'll carry this night in my memory forever." And he kissed her.

When Emma looked back, Angel had disappeared.

Emma Moment: *I am guided by divine light and interpret signs to understand my missions. I once thought this gift was a burden, but I do not feel like that anymore. I am me with it or without it, and everyone can accept me as I am. Una bruja bella. A beautiful witch.*

Good Luck Bath

Infused with nature's essences of cinnamon, mint, and honey, this bath will wrap you in abundance and prosperity. As you perform this ritual, allow its sweetness to attract good fortune and blessings into your life.

Ingredients:

- Seven stems of fresh Mint
- Three Cinnamon sticks
- 7 pieces of Cloves
- Your favorite Perfume
- A drop of Honey
- Holy water
- Florida water
- White candle
- Pot
- Bowl
- Colander
- Oven mitts

Directions:

1. Begin by filling a pot with water and boiling it on the stove.
2. Add seven stems of mint, three cinnamon sticks, and seven cloves to the water. Let it boil for 10 minutes or until the water deepens in color and the cinnamon sticks uncurl, releasing their essence.
3. Turn off the heat and allow the mixture to cool until lukewarm.
4. Place a colander over a bowl and carefully strain the mixture, using oven mittens to handle the pot safely. The herbs will be filtered out, leaving behind the infused water for your bath.
5. Once strained, add seven drops of honey to the water, stirring gently. Honey brings sweetness and attraction into your life.
6. Add a splash of holy water and a few drops of Florida water to the bowl, infusing it with sacred energy and spiritual protection.
7. Add a few drops of your favorite perfume, enhancing the bath with your essence and the energy you want to attract.
8. Light the white candle. Pass the candle over the bowl as you say aloud: ***"As I light this candle, I light this bath with abundance, good luck, and all sweetness, or whatever comes to your mind. In the divine light of the Holy Spirit, Amen."***
9. Using your hands, stir the water clockwise while focusing on your intentions. As you do so, say something like: ***"With this bath, I attract good***

fortune, creativity, and new opportunities, or whatever comes to your mind. In the name of God, or the One Force, or the One Source, Amen."

10. Set the bowl aside. Take your regular shower, cleansing your body and spirit in preparation for the ritual.

11. After your shower, take the bowl of prepared water and slowly pour it over your head and body, letting it cover you completely. As you do this, repeat your intentions aloud or whatever else comes to your mind, affirming your desires. You can end with: ***"In the name of God, or the One Force, or the One Source, Amen. Thank you."***

12. Allow the water to sit on your skin for 30 to 60 seconds, absorbing its energy.

13. Finally, gently towel dry.

Let this bath be a reminder that the universe always supports you. Use it as a tool to welcome luck into your life, open doors of opportunity, and fill your path with light and abundance. Trust in the process, and may your intentions manifest in beautiful and unexpected ways.

Emma's Pink Margarita Recipe

You can almost feel the warm breeze as you prepare Emma's Pink Margarita drink in her cozy apartment with the sun streaming through the windows. Gather the ingredients in the recipe listed below and follow the instructions to transport yourself to a tropical paradise right in the heart of the city. You can create this tropical drink while reading this book and following Emma's adventure. For non-alcoholic drinks, just keep the pink lemonade without alcohol.

Ingredients:

- 2 oz of your preferred margarita mix or pink lemonade.
- 1.5 oz of your favorite tequila
- 1/2 cup of ice (optional, for "on the rocks")
- Pink sea salt of your choice for rimming the glass.
- Margarita glass
- Lemon slice or a heart-shaped strawberry slice for garnish

Instructions:

1. Start by preparing your margarita glass. Gently rub a fresh lemon slice around the rim of the glass to moisten it.
2. Dip the moistened rim into a plate of pink sea salt you choose to create a beautiful pink salt rim. Set the glass aside.
3. In a blender, combine the margarita mix or pink lemonade, your favorite tequila, and ice (if you prefer "on the rocks").
4. Blend until the mixture is smooth and the ice is crushed to your desired consistency.
5. Pour the vibrant pink margarita into the prepared glass.
6. Garnish the drink with a thin lemon slice on the rim or a heart-shaped strawberry slice on the side of the glass for an extra touch of love and citrusy flavor.
7. Finish with "Salute to Emma's Pink Margarita!" and enjoy your refreshing drink.

ACKNOWLEDGMENTS

God, thank you! I woke up one morning remembering this dream and knew I had to write this book. Thank you to all my angels and spiritual guides for sprinkling magical ideas that weaved creativity throughout this book.

Thank you to my publisher, Tanya Anne Crosby, and editor extraordinaire Jill Stadler. I don't know how you have time to do what you do, but I couldn't be more grateful to have you both in my corner and for believing in the magic of this book. Thank you.

To my husband, I owe you many date nights.

To my kids, Aidan, and Ashley, when you have a vision, work hard, and success will come. This book is for both of you to believe in yourself.

To my sister, I truly appreciate your patience and support through countless calls and texts as I bounced story ideas, especially when you would say, "That's it, no more book talk." For believing in my vision and supporting me on this ride. You celebrated all of my wins as I celebrated yours.

To Linda Grindle, Psychic Medium (Linda G Comanche Psychic), Susan Lynn, Psychic Medium, and Kim Copeland, Intuitive Evidential Medium, thank you for all you do to keep us all calm. Linda, thank you for making all of us laugh and for your collaboration. Susan Lynn, for your helpful videos, I did what you said, and St. Michael helped me. Kim Copeland, for your beautiful light and crystals. Thank you, ladies.

I first found Sarra Cannon through her YouTube videos and her courses on Teachable. In her Facebook group, I connected with Sarah Fox and other amazing authors who helped me refine this book. It has been three years in the making, and it would not exist without Sarra's guidance and the generous support of the Publish and Thrive community. Thank you all for your insight and encouragement.

Thank you, Sarah Fox, and your team. Your assistance from the very beginning and your patience in answering all my questions have helped me immensely.

To all my social media family, your love and excitement for this book made this happen.

To all those who have a dream but are unsure how to make it happen:

One, it starts with a big dream.

Two, taking baby steps to learn and research your dream.

Three, by taking the risk and going for it, you get one step closer to seeing it, to holding it in your hands, and to visually seeing the end result.

To everyone who reads this book, I want to express my gratitude. This book came to life because of a dream I had with a divine message, "You are not alone. God and his angels are always around. When you feel alone, take a moment to ask aloud, and you will be surprised at how your life can change for the good."

From my humble heart, thank you!

Want to know more about Anita Fonteboa and what she is currently writing? Be on her ARC Team, then sign up for her newsletter. Be the first to know about new releases, giveaways, and more! Scan the QR code today or click the Flodesk link below!

Flodesk Newsletter: https://authoranitafonteboa.myflodesk.com/d3qhdvk5bc

Follow ***Anita Fonteboa's YouTube channel*** and listen to

Emma's Playlist that goes along with Book One in The Gift Series.

If this book touched you, I invite you to support the author by writing a short review on retailers' websites. Reviews help with the book's success, and your valuable opinion can make a huge difference in supporting her books. Thank you.

ABOUT THE AUTHOR

Anita Fonteboa is an intuitive psychic who weaves intuition and inspiration into every page, always with a plot twist or two. She writes fiction with fantasy, magic, and romance, where intuition meets imagination and the unexpected is always just a page away. She's also the author of three uplifting self-help books, including one released in Spanish. Whether she's crafting fiction or sharing new age insight through spiritual self-help, her books help readers reconnect with themselves and find moments of laughter.

When she's not writing, she's sipping a *cafecito*, watching Hallmark movies, or traveling to places that spark her next big idea. Listen to the Anita Inspires podcast on Apple Podcasts, Spotify, and more. Shop her merch store at https://anitain spires-shop.fourthwall.com.

Visit her website at https://anitafonteboa.com.
Facebook Fan Group:https://www.facebook.com/groups/fanta syandmiracles

Follow her on social media:

instagram.com/authoranitafonteboa

facebook.com/AuthorAnitaFonteboa

tiktok.com/@authoranitafonteboa

amazon.com/author/anitafonteboa

bsky.app/profile/anitafonteboa.bsky.social

bookbub.com/profile/anita-fonteboa

goodreads.com/anitafonteboa

linkedin.com/in/anitafonteboa

A small press bound by the belief that every voice matters.

Sign up for our newsletter to learn about new releases and
more.
https://oliver-heberbooks.com/subscribe/

Follow us on social media:

facebook.com/oliverheberbooks

instagram.com/oliverheberbooks

amazon.com/oliverheberbooks

youtube.com/@OliverHeberBooksPublisher